WARRIOR BLACK

Tone Deaf

Warrior Black Series
Book 3

CJ Barlowe

Tone Deaf Ebook Edition ISBN # 978-1-961685-13-0

Paperback Edition ISBN # 978-1-961685-14-7

Tone Deaf

1: Relatively insensitive to differences in musical pitch

2: Having or showing an obtuse insensitivity or lack of perception particularly in matters of public sentiment, opinion, or taste.

He who will not listen cannot learn.

~Harold S. Geneen

This book is for everyone whose voice has gone unheard. Keep shouting, keep speaking, keep reaching out—because we are listening. Your words matter.

Chapter One

C allum

The moment I step into the house on my three-acre mountain retreat, I'm able to breathe a sigh of relief. I bought this property with money from my cut of the first royalty check the band received. It was the second best damn decision I've made so far in my career—the first was agreeing to form Warrior Black with my best mates, Danny, Connor, Rafe and Bobby. They were the first kids to befriend me when my mum and I moved from Australia to the United States, and to this day we're still tight.

I love this time of the year in Colorado. The chilly March air, the thin layer of snow glistens in the bright sunshine. The mountains—with the still-green needles of their Colorado blue spruce, Douglas fir, and Ponderosa pine making it obvious why this town was named Evergreen. It can't be any more perfect.

The air is clean and woodsy smelling. My breathing is easy, even though the town is about seven thousand feet above sea level.

As I stand in my own private space, the tension headache I've been battling for the past few days begins to ease into nothing.

Don't get me wrong, I love being around my friends—being on the road—touring. But in the last two years, after Ron Darling became our manager, we've gone from a band playing local gigs to one that goes on tour, and have screaming fans at every stop.

And let's not forget the *invites* to music festivals like Rocktoberfest. We are going again in October—for the *third* time. Talk about a mind fuck. It hasn't been all rosy, though.

Our frontman, Danny *Raven* Wells, had a stalker right before our first trip to Rocktoberfest. Not only was that scary as fuck, but the band ended up with twenty-four hour security—and what an adjustment *that* was for five kids from the Chicago 'burbs. Then, as we were getting ready for our second year at Rocktoberfest, we had to deal with Connor's pedo-uncle's bullshit. Between the two dramas and touring, lately there has been more chaos than my anxiety can handle.

At least my mates don't give me any flak when I need to escape into solitude—they've known about my anxiety since we were kids. So, the guys are used to me disappearing from time to time.

However, the current upheaval in my life stems from my father—okay, maybe not just him. But Callum Brian Fitz, Senior—Brian to most, has been the bane of my existence as far back as I can remember. He's been even worse the last three months. His calls and texts have been a constant buzzing, like an annoying fly. No matter how often I tell Brian to fuck off, the man doesn't want to listen.

And yes, I call him by his middle name because he doesn't deserve my respect or the honor of being called Dad, or even Father.

The call I got from him two nights ago was the breaking point for me.

In the past, when Brian poured his negativity like molten metal, trying to scar me all the way down to my soul, I was able to ignore him and move on. For some reason, this last call hit me differently, even though the deep-rooted barbs he spewed weren't anything new.

According to Brian, I don't associate with the right people. My friends are degenerates. I won't go anywhere with my playing. My band's so-called music is loud and senseless. My appearance is far from presentable. And I'm gay.

Well, sorry to disappoint you, Brian. You can go fuck right off.

I'm proud of all those attributes—from my friends to the people I associate with. And the music? It's what saves my sanity from imploding. My life wouldn't be the same without the music that flows through my head and out my fingertips. The bright melodies bring color to the darker corners of my life. I guess a part of me—the ten-year-old kid I used to be—is still chasing Brian's approval. But the adult in me says *I don't give a fuck what he says... Much.*

My father is tone deaf to who I am as a person, as a gay man and as a rocker.

Brian might have donated the sperm, but he certainly isn't my dad. Not like Connor's dad, Markus Wild—our drummer's father was kind, respectful, supportive and just an all-around good human. He treated me as if I were his son, too. It was a dark day for our Wildman—for all of us, when Mr. Wild died four months ago.

I still feel the sting of the loss, almost like I'm the one who lost a father. It's as though one of the strings on my Fender Stratocaster snapped and the steel wire cut sharply across my heart. I'm not alone in this—we all loved Markus and his death created a seismic tremor whose aftershocks are still rippling through the band. It's taking us a bit to recapture our energy.

Brian's call wasn't the only reason why I left. The band decided to take a break after our eight-week U.S. tour, and we've each gone our separate ways, as we try to heal.

Danny is with Tobias and his dog, Scout, at the lake house. Connor and John are spending quality time with the Connor's mother. Bobby and Rafe said they were headed to Vegas, where our lead guitarist has a condo, along with their security, Fig and Jordan. We were all glad when Jordan rejoined our security team after a short sabbatical from the tour. Though, he's disposition has changed some. He's quieter—more reserved than before. But that's okay by me.

So here I am, slowly breathing in and out, as I gaze out the floor-to-ceiling window at the mountains.

Blow out the bad. Inhale the good. I repeat that mantra over and over until my mind clears and my body settles. I'm ready to hunker down, absorb the quiet and solitude this place affords me. With the tranquility the house radiates, I hope to write a few songs and enjoy the solitude.

After stowing my clothes and guitar away, I check the fireplace, making sure the flue is clean. Nothing would shatter my visit more than having a chimney fire. I pay a property management company to check my place, but you can't be too sure.

Seeing only unobstructed daylight in the flue, I light one

of those artificial logs in the fireplace. Once done, I uncork a bottle of one of my favorite pinots and fill a glass.

Glancing down at the dark liquid I'm swirling in the glass, my mind shifts to the night before last. To Brian's nasty call that drove me over the edge, which made me search for something harder than my usual pinot.

Remembering that Rafe had a bottle of Macallan fifty-year old single malt, I stole it from cabinet he hides it in, and nearly down myself in a eighth of the bottle to drown out the memory of Brian's words.

Once Rafe finds out, I hope he won't be mad at me.

It had worked, but it also numbed my resolve to stay distant from two of Warrior Black's bodyguards—Pennington Gallagher and Dominic Rossetti.

Dom's Italian descent is evident in his rich olive complexion. His sharp angular jawline, straight Roman nose, thick black hair and dark brown eyes make me melt every time he looks at me. He's a really hard man for me to say *No* to.

And Pen? I love his gorgeous bright smile, not-so-perfect nose, and his blond hair that's always pulled back into a short ponytail at the nape of his neck, beautiful Pen is everyone's vision of a surfer wet dream.

You see, Dom and Pen are a couple—discreet—but anyone who looks closely can see the pull between them. Even so, they are each attracted to me, and these men have no issues telling me so.

There's a quiet tension whenever we're together, and over in the last year, that energy has only grown. It was all innocent, and I didn't think so much on where these moments would lead me.

However, all my ambiguity aside, seven months ago Pen planted a sweet kiss on me that knocked my socks off. The following week, during one of the intermissions, Dom pulled me into an empty room and captured my mouth with a hungry want. I was hooked.

From kissing, we went to getting each other off, which has made some fucking fantastic moments of frotting between the three of us. But not once did they ever pressure me into getting fucked by them.

Until two nights ago. Between a belly full of scotch, my head full of Brian's foulness, I caved and we all gave in to our desires.

I slept with both men. My bodyguards—and don't even ask me how I ended up with two instead of one bodyguard like the rest of my bandmates.

With the two of them focused on me—on my body, it was mere moments before there was nothing in my head but Pen and Dom. I shiver at the memory of how they made my body sing.

Now though? I can only imagine the confusion that must have been on their faces when they woke the next morning and discovered my absence from their bed. Maybe I should have left a note for them, because I certainly don't want them to worry. But when Dom started talking about me joining them on their vacation to Cancun, and Pen used the word *relationship*, I panicked.

I'm not ready for a relationship with either of them, or both. I tried to refuse the trip, but Dom wouldn't take no for an answer... I'm back to my first thought—it's hard saying no to Dominic.

How do I explain to them that I made a mistake by sleeping with them? That I wasn't thinking clearly because I had used alcohol to exorcise Brian's cruel words from my head. Or how do I explain my insecurities about relation-ships? My lack of knowledge about how to navigate this complicated connection I feel for two people I have come to care about? That it doesn't matter if I've fallen in love with both of them. Because, in the end, all relationships go bad. Look at my parents and what my mother still has to endure from my narcissistic father.

No matter how much I want to be with Pen and Dom—in and out of bed, they won't ever find out about my true feelings for them both.

Knock. Knock. Knock. "Callum."

"What the..." I swivel my head toward the front door, hearing my name in a man's muffled voice as the knocking continues. I'm not expecting anyone... "No, it can't be Dom and Pen," I mutter to myself.

Dom knows where this house is—he came with me a few months ago when there'd been a break in. But he wouldn't have been sure I'm here unless, "Damn it, Danny," I hiss as I stride to the door, gathering my resolve to tell my security team that I don't need them. I'm not ready to face them yet— they are a distraction I can't have while I sort myself and this situation out.

Sure that it's one or both of them standing on my stoop, I don't bother to look through the side window to see who's here. I blindly whip open the door, and that's my mistake. One moment, I'm standing there, staring at the back of a stranger, their head covered by a hoodie, and the next thing I know, my face blooms with so much pain and I'm laid out on the floor.

"Tell Brian Fitz to keep his nose out of my fucking business or the next time you won't be breathing." Then whoever it is punches me again, and my vision explodes with stars.

He keeps punching. I cover my head with my arms, so he starts kicking me... and then everything goes black.

Chapter Two

D^{om}

"What do you mean, you don't know where Callum is?" I question Tobias, even though I already know where Callum ran to. His Colorado home. It's the only place that makes sense. But I want confirmation. Unfortunately, my lead is good at keeping his mouth shut. His face remains neutral on my phone's screen.

"Don't play games, Dom. You know damn well where Callum's at."

"I'm not playing games. I'm calling to confirm my hunch is right," I say as I glance over at Pen, who's frowning. "Tell me."

"All Danny said is that Callum needs time alone to think and to clear his head," Tobias says. "And I think it's wise for you to not go after him, Dom."

"Jesus Christ, Tobias," I rumble out in frustration. "How in the hell are we supposed to keep him safe if we aren't with him?"

"Are you sure that's your main goal? To keep him safe? Or is your intention on something else?"

I clench my teeth tight at that insinuation. Although the man isn't wrong. My—or our, need to see Callum is strictly personal. He crept out of our bed without a word, leaving Pen and me baffled, like we did something wrong. But I know we didn't.

"Where are you?" There's a note of warning in Tobias's tone.

I completely ignore his question. "We're his security, Tobias. If Danny did this—"

"I know," he says, cutting me off. He breathes out a sigh. "I'd be doing the same thing. Just that... Tell me that you are going to give him the time he needs."

"I already did. We just want him to say it out loud," I proclaim, my eyes never leaving Pen. He gives me a subtle nod in agreement.

"We? Who's we—and where are you?"

"Pen and I are at a bar," I lie. Sort of. We *were* at a bar—specifically, in one of the executive lounges at LAX, killing time before our flight. But that was hours ago. Now we're standing inside at Denver International, waiting for the bus to take us to the parking lot where we pick up our rental car.

"Rossetti," he growls.

"Gotto go. Call you later." I hang up before Tobias presses for more answers.

After we talk sense into Callum and explain to the bassist that Pen and my feelings are genuine, we three will unwind and recharge for a week before we leave his mountain home.

Pen frowns. "Tobias was no help."

"No, but he does know where Callum is. And so do I."

The moment the bus pulls up, we step outside and the chilly air hits my face.

"But what if..." Pen starts and pauses. He has a faraway look, a layer of doubt furrowing between his brows. "I don't want to push Callum into something he doesn't want, Dom."

For as fierce and confident as Pen is while working a security detail, when it comes to personal relationships, he has a habit of thinking too much—then doubt filters in and his insecurities—most of which are caused by his family, get in the way.

I turn to Pen, his anxious eyes meeting mine. "I *know* he wants us. And the other night proved it."

"I agree," he says, although doubt laces his voice.

Does he? Because I'm as sure of that as I am of wanting Pen from the day I laid my eyes on the man.

When it became clear that Danny had a stalker, Ron contacted Harper Security, and Dean Harper assigned Tobias and John to Warrior Black. As the threats escalated, Dean assembled the rest of our team—Fig, Jordan, Pen and me. The day before we left for San Francisco to begin the job, I knew that Pen would be in my life. Pen says the same about me.

Neither of us had been in a relationship before, and it took a while for us to connect. We were professionals, and working together made it more complicated. But we agreed to be careful and discreet. However, by the comments the band and the rest of our team make, our attempts at discretion have not been wildly successful—especially when we "allowed" ourselves to be talked into sharing a bedroom when Ron deemed the band to be safer if everyone moved into the mansion together.

We never planned to add a third—that kind of snuck up

on us. Despite our strong feelings for each other, we both found we also want Callum. However, we don't want to fuck it all up by pushing Callum into a throuple if he doesn't want to be with us. But that's the wild hair. Callum does.

I see it in his eyes when he looks at us. The desire. The need.

The way we three connected when we loved each other for the first time the other night, there's now no doubt in my mind that we fit like three perfect puzzle pieces.

Then Pen used the word *relationship*, and Callum freaked out. It didn't help that his asshole father had called him earlier. It spurred Callum to run from us. Every time that son of a bitch calls, Pen and I have to pull Callum out of his head and the blackness that swims in his thoughts. We try to intercept those calls, but we can't catch all of them. Brian Fitz is a plague to his son, and I'd love to wipe him clean from this earth.

We can be his solace—his safe space. But there's something there... His old man has a hold on him that prevents Callum from reaching out to us. I just need to figure out what it is.

"I'm not going to sit still and wait for the bass player to make a decision on if he wants us or not. We agreed to this, Pen."

"What if Callum rejects us? All he has to say are those simple words, and then we have no choice but to comply with his wishes."

"He won't," I reaffirm.

"I don't know if I can keep working for Warrior Black knowing my heart..." His voice chokes up.

I get close, gripping the back of Pen's neck. "Look at me," I command, and he swings his eyes from the ground up to mine. "From the moment we realized that we both felt something for Callum, we wanted him with us. Am I right?"

He nods slowly. "Yeah."

"Then don't let doubt fill your head. Focus on how good we are when we three are together. Okay?" I squeeze his neck when the silence between us grows. "Pen."

"You're right." He takes a breath, and then steps away from me. "You know it's going to take us close to an hour to get there from here."

I kiss him gently, both of us needing the connection, before pulling back and looking into his green eyes. "I'm telling you, we're not that far behind. Callum left on the first flight out early this morning—I'm sure of it," I say, releasing him, then reaching down and hefting the bag over my shoulder. "There's the shuttle to get to our rental car."

Without further encouragement, we climb in the crowded bus. The drive to the lot takes fifteen minutes and it's a welcome reprieve when we get off the transport. The multiple body odors and the mix of perfumes—all strong—mingling in the air, causing an overload to my senses.

Once the fresh air clears my head, we track down the dark blue Bronco. We load our things into the back of the vehicle and leave the lot.

Getting on I-70 is a breeze, but we're jammed up in traffic through downtown Denver. After we pass the city limits, the drive turns easier. Finally, about an hour and a half later, we pull into Callum's driveway.

I was here once before and was blown away. The place is amazing—five bedrooms, each with an en suite bathroom, a game room, a professional kitchen, floor-to-ceiling windows in the huge living room, and a deck, a hot tub, an in-ground pool, and a fire pit in the back. Now I'm watching for Pen's reaction.

Through the thinning pine trees, the house doesn't look imposing. But as we drive closer, the bigger the home stands against the mountain backdrop. From the way Pen's eyes are nearly popping out of his head, he is as shocked as I was to see how beautiful Callum's retreat home is.

"I didn't know," Pen mumbles.

"Neither did I, until I came here with him after the break in," I admit.

Pen lowers the window half way and sucks in the clean mountain air. "I can get used to this."

I'd have to agree, taking in the view. From this angle, I'm partly facing the Rocky Mountain range. I'm excited for Pen to see the back of the house and the deck.

"Before we unload the luggage, I want to surprise Callum first," I say with a smile, putting the vehicle into park in front of the four-car detached garage.

We walk around a gigantic boulder on the corner of the side yard, then follow the walkway to the front door—which is wide open. My stomach drops when my eyes land on Callum's still form, lying on the floor in the doorway. For a second I think—he's dead.

"Fuck. Callum." Pen's shout yanks me out of that horrible thought. We move fast and drop onto the floor next to Callum. "Dom, his face."

"Call 911." I check for his pulse. "It's strong," I inform Pen without looking at him.

"Jesus. He looks like someone used his face as the punch dummy," Pen grates out.

"Call the fucking cops, Pen." I glare up at him.

"I am," he fires back, nostrils flared and mouth in a snarl.

I drop my eyes back to Callum, who remains motionless. I lean in and examine his face more thoroughly. His nose doesn't look broken, but there's a ton of blood. His left eye is swollen shut; there's a gash on his lips and scrape marks on his cheeks. Whoever did this to Callum is in a world of hurt, once I get my hands on the son of a bitch.

Callum groans, his right eye slowly opens, and I see the white of his eye is all bloodshot.

"Dom?" he whispers, like I'm an illusion. He reaches a hand to my face but it falls before he can touch me and he whimpers.

"I'm here, baby," I choke out, trying to swallow down the knot at the base of my throat.

"Is that really you?"

"Don't move, sweetheart, the cops are on the way." I place a hand on his cheek. "Who attacked you?"

He closes his eye, slowly shakes his head and let out a groan of pain. "I didn't see his face. But it was a guy who..."

"A guy? Are you sure it was a man?" I growl low, rage filtering through my words even though I'm trying to keep him calm.

"Yes. He called me by name."

"Hey," Pen says, the cell phone still to his left ear. He takes Callum's uninjured hand, raises it and kisses his knuckles. "The ambulance is on its way. Just hold on a little longer, sweetheart."

"My father..."

"What about your father?" Pen asks gently, but he can't hide the disdain on his face.

"He said... Brian..." Callum swallows hard and then chokes out a cry.

"If Brian has anything to do with this—I promise you, he will pay and the fucker who hurt you will too," Pen conveys softly, but his face holds a wealth of fury.

A small smile sneaks across Callum's face before he passes out.

"Callum," I shout, before hearing sirens in the distance. The sound puts my teeth on edge, as it stirs old memories, but it also sends a measure of relief through me, knowing he will be getting help soon.

It's a scramble of lights, sounds, and uniformed officers running around us. As I stand there helplessly and watch an EMT work on Callum, the fire of revenge is flowing through my veins like lava. I have to keep telling myself that Callum is in good hands.

"I'm going to see if Callum set up the security surveillance we recommended after the break in," Pen whispers to me, before leaving my side.

His words jolt me out of my red haze and I follow him through the house. If he did, I know for a fact they will have captured the attacker.

Technically, we shouldn't be inside the home at all, since it's a crime scene now, but neither of us gives a shit. Pen and I are on the same wavelength—we need to see who attacked Callum and get to them first, before the cops.

"I swear, Dom, if Brian has anything to do with Callum's attack—"

"I know," I say, trying to remain calm for both our sakes.

As we go through the house, we see that the interior is untouched. It tells me this wasn't an ordinary attack, and for sure not a burglary attempt.

"Head straight back," I say, pointing toward the back of the house.

Pen quickly finds the office, except we're met with absolute calamity. Callum had apparently listened to us and had the surveillance and cameras set up around the property, but the security equipment is trashed. The computer monitors are smashed and so are the two storage towers that hold the recordings.

"What the fuck?" Pen hisses. "How did they know?"

"Whoever did this is smart. The bastard had to have been watching Callum for a while to even know he was here. And he made sure to cover up his tracks," I say as I use my left foot to move one of the busted monitors. "Let's get out of here. I don't want shit from the cops for messing with the evidence."

Pen agrees and we are both heading back out to see how Callum is doing, when two detectives approach us with wary looks marring their faces.

"I'm Detective Jacob Longe and this is Detective Alaric Faller. We need to ask you two a few questions."

After they separate Pen and me, the questions begin. Since they already know we've been in the house, there's nothing to hide. So I explain quickly and plainly. I want to get back to Callum, who is still lying on the floor while the EMTs set up the gurney.

However, my explanation is apparently not clear enough because Longe repeats the same questions. But I know this tactic well; I used it when I worked for the U.S. Marshals many years ago. So once again I explain, but then quickly put a halt on the questioning when Longe asks me to go over what happened for the third time.

As I walk away from Longe, the EMTs are bracing Callum's neck. They ease him onto a body board, then lift and secure him to the gurney. Straps click into place before they wheel him to the ambulance.

"Where are you taking him?" I demand as an EMT secures the gurney Callum's laying on inside the ambulance.

"Lutheran General," one of the EMTs calls out before he shuts the back doors and climbs into the driver's seat. They take off, lights on and sirens blaring.

"I have more questions, Mr. Rossetti," Longe says as he blocks my view of the ambulance.

"No, you don't. You've asked twice already. I know the game, Detective, and I'm done playing." I'm frustrated with the repeated questions, and restless. I need to follow the ambulance to the hospital.

"Just one more," the detective says with a frown. "You mentioned Mr. Fitz was the victim's father."

"Callum Brian Fitz Senior. Callum says the attacker mentioned him. It's all I know. Then Callum passed out before he said anything else."

"And you and this other man are Mr. Fitz's bodyguards?" The detective's tone suggests that he doesn't believe me.

"Yes," I bite out. "Callum Fitz is the bassist for the rock band Warrior Black. We," I point between Pen and me, "*are* Mr. Fitz's security team."

"Then why weren't you two with your charge? Was there a fight between you three?"

"Am I under arrest?" I demand, disregarding the detective's last question, which surprises the man.

"No, but..."

"Then if there's nothing more, Pen Gallagher and I are heading to the hospital."

As I turn my back on Longe, he grunts out, "Wait." I pause, ready to continue this verbal battle, when the detective hands me a business card. "Don't leave town. We will have more questions for you later."

"Will do." I whistle, grabbing Pen's attention as I stride toward our rental. He catches up with me, looking as frustrated with Detective Faller as I am with Longe. He strides over to me. "We're going to the hospital."

"Detective Faller is a giant dick," he spits out as he climbs into the Bronco. "He kept repeating the same question— asking just a little differently—like I'm some fucking idiot

who doesn't know what he's doing. And his accusatory tone—
I wanted to punch the asshole."

"Same," I agree as I start the vehicle.

Silence fills the space for a long moment, before I say what we both are thinking. "We have to call Tobias."

"I'm not looking forward to it," Pen imparts with a frown.

I groan. "And I thought we had finally settled back into the easy work." Meaning, after the whole shitstorm that went down with Connor and his deviant uncle six months ago, I thought this year was going to be smooth.

"Maybe we should call Dante first," Pen suggests. "They are, after all, the band's manager."

Dante Ross hasn't been with the band long, not even a year. They were hand-picked by Ron to take over for him when he started his cancer treatment. Dante's proven they're capable, but they are prickly. I rarely initiate a conversation with them.

"Tobias will take the news better," I say as I tap the screen on my cell phone for our lead's contact, while trepidation and worry for Callum churns and settles heavy in my gut.

Please be okay.

Chapter Three

P en

I pace in the emergency waiting room while Dom remains outside, making more calls. I can't believe the hospital staff— namely the nurse at the emergency room desk, won't allow me or Dom in the room with Callum. Even though we showed her our credentials and explained how we are his bodyguards, she still refused us entry.

Dom strides back inside, a scowl carved deep across his face. "Tobias, the rest of the team and the band, along with Dante, are on their way. So are some of Dean's men that he is pulling off of other jobs."

"Why?" I ask, since Harper Security isn't currently employed by Warrior Black or LC Records. Dom and I used to work for Dean—as did the rest of the band's current security team.

However, once Tobias and John became romantically involved with two of the band members, they left Harper Security and formed their own group solely to provide security for Warrior Black. Not much later, Fig joined them. Then Jordan not long after that. Dom and I both took a permanent sabbatical a year ago to be on tour with the band, and Dean knows we aren't coming back.

As if those defections from Harper Security weren't enough, Ron swayed the band's label to hire Tobias's new team and terminate the contract with Dean Harper. So the fact that Dean is sending men raises all kinds of questions.

"Dante brought him in—or should I say Ron made the choice. They think we aren't handling the security properly and want Dean's input," Dom growls.

"That's bullshit," I grunt out. "What does Tobias say?"

"Tobias isn't happy either that Dante pulled Dean into this, but he has no say. Dante has the backing of the record label's higher-ups."

I expel a long exhale, contemplating what kind of conflict will ensue when Tobias and Dean go head-to-head on this matter. "All I care about right now is if Callum is okay—Christ! I can't stand here and not know if he needs us," I blurt out.

Nurse Ratchet at the desk stares at me with open hostility, but I don't give a fuck. I open my mouth to tell her to shove it, but Dom holds up a hand to shut me up. He walks over to the desk, leans in and whispers something, and her face goes pale and she starts nodding.

Dom turns, grins wide at me and says, "Let's go."

"What did you say to the woman?"

"I told her that if something happens to Callum while we're out here, it's going to be her ass and her job on the line. The lawsuit we'll bring down on the hospital will be nothing compared to what she will lose," he says with a grin.

I chuckle. "Dom does it again."

I follow him down the wide corridor, peeking between the curtains, until we come to the last cubicle on the left. Dom sweeps open the curtain that separates the space from the walkway, and there, lying in the bed, is Callum. An IV is hooked up to his right arm—but his left arm is in a splint. A heart monitor bleeps in the background and the blood pressure cuff is wrapped around his biceps groans and expands.

He also has a nasal canula in his nostrils for oxygen. His poor face has been cleaned and a few of the scrapes have been bandaged, and his nose is taped across the bridge... But the swelling... *Jesus Christ.*

My heart aches at the sight of this beautiful, sweet man, unconscious and injured. Even though my trepidation about his feelings for us is a warning to check my emotions, my affection for the bass player grows stronger every time I'm with him. I just wish I knew what was going through Callum's head when he left us and if he'll ever want to be with Dom and me.

"Jesus." I walk over to the left side of the bed, while Dom moves to the right. We each tentatively touch a hand. "Who in the hell could have done this to him?" I look to Dom for answers.

"I don't know, babe. But fuck, I promise you I'll find out who's behind Callum's attack."

"If you two are going to remain in here, you need to be quiet and stop swearing. We have sick kids that can hear all this. You're talking loudly, and it isn't helping them or their parents." A male nurse stands by the curtain. Despite being shorter than Dom and me, the glare he levels at us is fierce. "Now, I need to take Mr. Fitz's vitals, so please stand aside."

"You know who we are?" Dom's pointed glower at the nurse is equally stern. My eyes drop down to the name badge clipped to the nurse's dark blue scrub shirt. It reads Lyric. *Unusual.*

"I do." Lyric lifts his chin in defiance.

"Then you know who he is," Dom pushes.

"I do," Lyric repeats, his unnaturally blue—almost violet, almond-shaped eyes home in on Callum. "He's the bassist for the rock band, Warrior Black. I'm a fan."

"Then, you know what happened to Mr. Fitz, and why we have to take extra precautions on who comes in here," Dom explains firmly.

"Yes." Lyric's jaw tenses as he shifts the electronic note book from his right arm to his left. "But that's not my call. You need to take it up with the head charge nurse and the head of security."

"A call has been made. But I want to be perfectly clear with you, until Mr. Fitz leaves this hospital, you are the only nurse that will be able to enter his room."

"But..." The nurse's eyes widen in surprise, then narrow seconds later. He's not happy to hear that order. "I need to talk to Mrs. Gavin, she's in charge."

"That's fine," Dom continues, not caring if the nurse likes his command or not. "Now which doctor will be tending to Mr. Fitz?" Dom's eyes never waver from Lyric's face.

"Dr. Monroe is on staff in the emergency room," he says, then adds, "Now, can you let me do my job?"

Dom glances at me, nods and then we both step away from the bed. We watch the nurse as he checkmarks his name on the dry erase board on the wall. He then looks over Callum's IV and the fluid bags—and the lines that connect to Callum's arm, and then taps something on his electronic pad. After Lyric registers the blood pressure, he adds more notes.

"We would like to talk to Dr. Monroe," I say evenly. There's no need for me to be demanding, since Dom is doing enough of that. Lyric starts shaking his head, but I cut him off. "Reason being, in the next few hours, this emergency room will be inundated with more security and the rest of the band. Trust me, you would rather have us give them the diagnoses in the waiting room than have them badgering you in here."

The nurse sighs in resignation. "Give me five minutes."

"Thank you," I say with a smile.

His eyes drop to my mouth for a beat. I'm not sure if Lyric realizes how hungrily he's staring at me. There's a sudden heat at my back, and the nurse's eyes shift to Dom behind me, before he spins around and leaves.

I turn my head and smirk. "Jealous?" I ask huskily.

"Want me to be?" he says before nipping at my ear. "It's okay that he appreciates you from afar, as long as there's no touching what is mine."

"That's not fair." Callum's croaky voice has Dom and me whirling around and rushing to the bed.

"Hey," I say, and gently take Callum's hand.

"What happened?" Callum asks as he slowly moves his eyes around the room.

"Don't you remember?" Dom asks as he leans in and kisses Callum's forehead.

Callum tries to shake his head, but groans in pain from the movement. "My brain hurts."

"I bet it does," Dom says softly. "Someone attacked you."

Callum becomes so still, as if moving would bring about the apocalypse. The hand I'm holding tightens into a vise before he says, "I don't—Yeah... I remember something now. A guy attacked me."

"You didn't see his face?" I ask softly.

"No, I didn't see who. At least I think I didn't—I can't remember. Everything in my head is a blur."

"That's okay. I'm just glad we got there in time and found you," Dom says with some measure of relief. But his tone belies what he and I are truly feeling. We are furious.

Not five minutes later, Dr. Monroe comes into the room. The older man spares us a glance before looking at Callum. "Mr. Fitz, I'm glad to see you are awake."

"How bad are my injuries?" Callum asks with hesitation.

"Well... Your left arm has a hairline. Your nose is broken. The x-rays came back and I'm glad to say that the orbital area around your eyes is intact, but no doubt you're concussed. You'll be swollen for a while, along with the black and blue bruising. I have scheduled you for a CT scan and an MRI for additional evaluation."

"He's being admitted?" Dom questions.

"Yes," Dr. Monroe conveys without looking at my partner.

"For how long?" I ask, taking a step closer to the doctor. I can't stand when a person doesn't look me straight in the eyes. It feels distrusting.

"Overnight—maybe two. It'll depend on what the other tests show." Dr. Monroe finally glances at me, and sneers before he departs the room.

"What the hell?" I turn to Dom, hoping he also saw what I saw from the doctor's strange behavior. "Did you see that?"

"Yeah," he admits and returns his attention to Callum, who's groaning. "Are you in pain?"

"My face and arm hurt," he admits.

Right then, Lyric walks back into the room with two syringes.

"What're in those?" Dom rasps out, stepping in front of Lyric right before the nurse reaches the IV stand.

"One is for pain and the other for infection," Lyric explains, his nostrils flaring with irritation. "Want me to test it out on you first?" He points the capped syringe in Dom's direction, and my boyfriend quickly moves out of the nurse's way.

"No thank you," Dom grates out. He might be a big man, but where needles are concerned, Dom is a scared little boy.

As Lyric drains the syringes into the IV, he tells Callum, "I've also added something for the nausea, in case the meds make you feel sick."

"Thank you," Callum whispers.

"Yeah, thank you," I say, but my eyes remain on Callum, whose body relaxes into the bed as he falls asleep.

"I notified hospital security and the charge nurse at the front desk of the impending horde coming in for Mr. Fitz. Hopefully, he'll be in a room by then," Lyric tosses over his shoulder as he leaves.

I glance at Dom, who is staring at the curtained doorway.

"He's a feisty one. Whoever snatches him up will have their hands full," Dom says, finally cracking a small smile before returning his serious attention to Callum.

I agree with a soft chuckle.

We remain in the emergency room with Callum until hospital staff arrive to take him for his CT scan. Dom goes with him while I wait. Soon after, a porter comes to take me up to the room where they'll bring Callum after the imaging.

Four and a half hours later, an already long and stressful day gets worse when the room is bombarded by the rest of Warrior Black and their security team. Then it becomes a fuck-of-a-lot worse when Callum's father shows up, and all hell breaks loose.

Chapter Four

Callum

I wake up to chaos. Shouts reach my ears, and I have no choice but to open my eyes—or try to, anyway, because they still feel swollen and it hurts to blink. I peer through slits at the blurry images before me.

After blinking slowly several times, I finally clear away the fuzziness and see who's doing all the yelling. My damn father, and Danny. They're facing off like two stubborn rams, ready to head-butt each other, all the while the security team is standing there—along with my bandmates, watching them.

"You have no right to be here. I know for a fact that Callum doesn't want to see you—not after the last phone call he got from you," Danny hisses, his face all red and his man-bun coming loose from the back of his head.

"I'm his father—you, on the other hand don't have a say

on what my son wants or needs," Brian counters, but it's a weak point. I might be his son by blood but Brian's far from being a father figure in my eyes.

Danny is right, though. The last person I want to see right now is this jag-off.

"What the hell is going on?" I croak out in a whisper, looking between Brian and Danny. But no one is paying me any attention. I glance at Tobias, then Dom and Pen's backs—they are positioned at the end of the bed like two protective sentinels. "Please?" I stress a little louder, feeling a tight ache in my throat.

Finally, I get everyone's attention and they all swivel their heads my way.

"Callum," Pen says, relief settling across his face as he reaches my side.

"Why are you shouting?" I ask, but my attention goes to Dom on my other side for the answer. I don't know why I'm seeking his guidance. But lately, I've been looking to Dom—and sometimes Pen for... Reassurance? I don't know.

"Your father stormed in here demanding—" Danny begins.

"I have every right to—" Brian barks.

"Fuck you do," Danny shouts back. "You have no right to be here, not after all the years of—"

I shoot my uninjured hand up—the one with the IV line, to cut off Danny's rising voice. "Danny, please," I croak out in a plea.

"I'm sorry." Remorse coats my friend's voice. He squeezes past Pen and smiles sadly at me. "How are you feeling?"

I take a moment to analyze myself, and the pain radiating from my face and my arm. "I hurt... my face especially." Right down to my eyeballs.

"I want everyone out of here," Brian booms out. "My son doesn't need—"

"That's a good idea." A man standing in the doorway interrupts Brian. He walks in, dressed in blue scrubs. "And it starts with you, sir." He points to Brian.

Thank you. Brian's shouting is adding to the pounding in my head.

"Who the hell are you to tell me what to do?" Brian leans toward what I assume is a nurse and snarls. It's his strategy to intimidate. Brian has done that to me and to my mum for most of my life.

"Back off or I'll show you what exactly what I can do." The beautiful nurse raises a hand and huffs, before smoothing down the front of his scrub shirt. "I'm Lyric, Mr. Fitz's nurse. And if you don't quiet down, I'll have you thrown out of the hospital quicker than you can shout *spit*, and you will not be able to enter again. Understand me, sir?"

"Damn," Rafe mumbles quietly in awe, but I still hear him.

"But I'm his family," Brian argues, calmer now. "They are not."

I slowly look around at my bandmates —my best friends since I was a kid, and at the security team I've known since we started this journey into the rock world. I glance at the familiar looking nurse and say, "He's wrong. These people are my family." Then I realize the one person I want to see isn't here. "Where's Mum? Danny and Mum are the only ones on my emergency contact list." I glare—or try to, at Brian.

He doesn't meet my eyes. "She's at home," he says with cold frankness. "I answered your mother's phone—and thank God, too."

I blink. "Why didn't she come?" But I know the answer before he speaks, and it makes an ache bloom in my chest.

"She doesn't need to see you in this... condition," he says, waving his hand toward me as though I'm an inconvenience.

"You didn't tell her I'm in the hospital, did you?" My voice, scratchy and weak from pain, still crackles with ire. But I know the truth from the pinched expression in the corner of his eyes. "You didn't tell her that I was hurt?"

"Trust me—"

"But I don't trust you," I say bluntly, giving him a dose of his own medicine. "Not after this. What are you into now, Brian?"

"What are you talking about?" There's confusion in his eyes, but I'm not buying it.

"This," I say hoarsely, pointing at my face. "Your shit is bringing trouble to my doorstep."

I try to sit up, but Pen lays a hand on my shoulder. "Don't move."

Lyric claps his hands to get everyone's attention. "You all can go to the waiting room down the hall right now. I'm only allowing two at a time in Mr. Fitz's room." He huffs, then looks at Dom before continuing. "And since his bodyguards won't leave, then only two more of you can stay." He raises a finger. "However, if there are any more disturbances in here, I'll be calling hospital security and I'm going to kick everyone out—I don't care who it is." Then Lyric folds his arms across his chest and slides a brook-no-argument frown onto his face.

"The nurse is right. Dom and Pen will remain here for protection" Tobias nods at them, "and Bobby and Mr. Fitz senior can stay. The rest of us will head to the waiting room."

Danny gasps, and pulls out a stick of gloss and slathers his lips as he glares up at his boyfriend.

"For a few minutes only," Tobias adds and leads my friends out of the room.

"Cool," Bobby says, talking around a sucker stick protruding from the corner of his mouth.

My eyes slide to Rafe, who's standing there, like he's frozen in place. His eyes are on the nurse like he's the Martin D-18E that Kurt Cobain played at the height of his career. The ultimate prize for my friend and the ultimate, near-impossible bucket list item he's trying to attain.

I want to chuckle at the look on my friend's face, but I hurt too much to let out a laugh.

Rafe has no idea what he's getting into if he wants to hook up with that nurse. I bet Lyric would lead him on such a crazy chase that my friend wouldn't know what hit him.

"Rafe," Connor snaps out over his shoulder.

Rafe's eyes jump to our drummer, then to me, and back to Lyric again before he stalks out of the room with a frown. His and Bobby's security guys, Fig and Jordan, follow right behind Rafe.

Fig announces from the doorway, "We'll stand outside the room and wait."

"Yep," Bobby says with a thumbs up.

"This is your final warning, Mr. Fitz. You need to keep your voice down." Lyric points a no-nonsense glare at him. The nurse then walks over to the side of the bed and quickly checks on me. "Are you in pain?"

"Yeah, a bit," I admit with a slight groan. Although I'm happy that the room has quieted down.

"Here." Lyric lifts a small, wired rectangular remote that's connected to my IV stand, and he places it in my good hand. "This will administer a dose of pain meds into the IV. Just push the button and in a few seconds, you'll start feeling it work."

"Could he overdose if he presses too many times?" Dom asks softly as he observes the IV line.

"No, it's timed. One push for every four hours." Then Lyric looks at me, "If the pain reliever isn't working, let me know and I can call the doctor and ask him for something stronger."

"Okay." I then press the button, and the pain almost immediately begins to slowly ebb away. "Thank you."

"If you need anything else, use the call button on your remote." Lyric places it next to my hand and smiles. He slides a narrowed-eyed frown to Dom and Pen, and a glare at Brian before walking out of the room.

Dom and Pen remain on alert, standing as sentries, as Brian approaches me. "Cal—"

"Dude, your face," Bobby interjects, his lips in a full frown. He isn't one for blood—or anything to do with bodily fluids. I'm surprised he didn't pass out when he came in here. "You really do look like shit."

"Thank you, Captain Obvious," I slur, feeling more of the effect of the pain meds flooding my system, and I yawn.

"I'm glad you're okay. But dude..." Bobby's forehead has a light sheen, and he can't look me straight in the face. He's going to be sick.

"Thanks. Now go before you puke all over me," I say to my friend. And without another word, Bobby bolts out of the room.

"Son." Brian steps around Dom. His eyes, which look exactly like mine, are glazing over, like he actually cares.

Even doped up, I know better. Still, I'm actually taken aback at the sudden emotion I see in my father. And just as fast as it arose, the split second of concern fades and leaves the bastard I know him to be front and center.

"I don't know where you come up with this shit, but you

can't blame me for your attack. I'm glad your mother isn't here to see you like this. I told you that your poofter ways were going to put you six feet under."

I struggle to get my brain cells in order. I only want to do this once. "The guy called out your name. He said *Brian Fitz.* So I'm asking again, what shady shit are you in?"

Dom steps in front of Brian and gets in his face. "You best answer his question," he snarls.

"But I'm not *in* anything shady." Brian's mouth gapes open, like he has more excuses to throw at me. Then he glances at Dom's hard expression and Brian quickly snaps it shut.

"I'm sure the cops will be real interested in knowing you had something to do with your son's attack," Pen adds with a shake of his head.

Dom shifts to the right and I'm able to see Brian's face. His wide eyes shift from Dom to me. "Callum, don't you see that I'm trying to—"

I cut him off, not wanting to hear more of his bullshit. "There's nothing you can say that I want to hear. You're not a part of my life anymore. You can leave and never come back. And I'll be changing my number so don't bother calling me."

Dom slots his muscular frame between the bed and my father again. "You heard him."

I look away. The constricting pain in my body continues to ease as the drugs in my system take full effect. However, it doesn't numb the ache in my heart my father has caused me. I close my eyes, hoping sleep will find me.

"You can leave, Mr. Fitz," Pen barks out, backing up Dom.

"I'm not—"

"Don't lie," Dom warns. "Or I'll call that nurse back, and

he and hospital security can put you out for good. What'll it be?"

I force my eyes open and see Dom doesn't wait for Brian to make a decision and hustles my father backward until he is out in the hall.

Pen closes the door and then returns to my side. He reaches for my hand and gently holds it. "Dom's going to call the detectives who are on your case. I'm sure they will want to know about your father's involvement. And I promise you Brian Fitz won't bother you again."

I squeeze Pen's hand and smile up at him. "Thanks." Then I close my eyes again and try to ward off the negativity, but it's too late. To know that my father is involved in my attack slashes my heart to pieces, and I'm bleeding internally.

I don't understand why Brian bothered to come. Was it just to throw more insults at me? To see the results of his handy work? Yet, his actions don't make sense... or is it the drugs in my system? Trying to put his visit out of my head, I cling to Pen's warm hand and let the numbness from the drugs lull me to sleep.

Chapter Five

It's taking everything in me to not take a swing at Brian Fitz. The bastard has done enough damage to his son's psyche. And to his face and body, if Callum heard correctly.

I spin him around instead, pushing him back against the wall with my forearm across his neck, my face inches from his. "Now tell me what shit you're in that got Callum hurt."

"I'm not—"

"Don't lie," I growl low. I'm getting tired of repeating myself with this asshole.

"I'm the only one who sees the truth in all this," Brian rushes out, puffs of his sour breath hitting my face.

"The only truth I want is the trouble you pushed onto your son."

"Are we having an issue here?" Lyric asks in a tone that's far from friendly. "Do I need to call security?"

I step back, dropping my arm. "No trouble."

Brian whips his head around and glares at the male nurse. "No, I was just leaving." He steps back with a parting shot to me. "I'll be seeing you around." He then strides away.

"Do I need to add him to the list of people not welcome back to Mr. Fitz's room?" Lyric's voice isn't quite as tight.

"Yes."

"Mr..." Lyric begins to say.

"Just Dom," I correct, looking down at the shorter man.

He's quite pretty—I noticed his looks when he was eyeing Pen in the ER. He has creamy flawless skin and those interesting violet eyes, which he's thinly lined in black to accentuate their shape. I can see why Rafe is rattled by Lyric's beauty.

One would also assume, from looking at the man, that Lyric is gentle in nature. But appearances can lie. I know firsthand how fierce Lyric can be with his verbal banter. He holds his own.

"Do you need extra security posted here?" His question jolts me out of my thoughts.

I clear my throat, glance down at the hallway and say, "We have it covered."

"Alrighty." Lyric shrugs and goes behind the nurses' station.

I head back to Callum's room, walk in quietly, and see Callum is sound asleep. Soft noises from the bathroom draw my attention and I hear Pen on the phone, talking with someone.

A few minutes later he comes out, a frown on his face. I lift a brow, conveying my unspoken question.

"That was Detective Faller. He and Longe are coming to

talk with Callum. He said he only called out of courtesy—do you believe that? Anyway, they'll be here soon," Pen explains, his eyebrows furrowing deeply in agitation. "Couldn't they have waited another day?"

"The attack is still fresh in Callum's mind. He might have details he could forget the longer they wait. Then we can tell them about Brian."

"Who are you telling about Brian?" Danny asks as he and Connor walks in.

"The cops," Pen relays, his eyes never leaving me.

"Good. Hopefully, they can track down who hurt Callum, and throw his ass in jail," Connor grates out indignantly.

"Hope so," Danny says, equally angry. "What if it's not because of Brian?"

Danny makes a good point. "If it's not because of something Brian did, then who would want Callum hurt? Any grudges—does he have enemies we don't know about?" I ask, trying to make sure we have all avenues covered.

Danny drops into the chair that sits adjacent to the bed. "Tobias asked the same questions. And the answers are *I don't know* and *No*. Callum isn't the type to create enemies. But his father... Let's just say Brian is a piece of shit. Especially to Callum."

"We know all about Brian's foul mouth, but how does this pertain to Callum's attack? There are no connecting dots," Pen says, reaching my side.

"Don't quote me and I don't know details, but I remember overhearing my parents talking about Brian and the shady shit he did back in Australia. Right, Connor?"

"You got that right. Brian Fitz is a parasite," the drummer rumbles out with disdain.

"What's the shady shit?" I ask, needing to know how far

Fitz senior would go to hurt Callum. "Would he purposefully have his own son hurt?"

Both band members glance at each other before Danny refocuses on me and says, "I wouldn't put it past the bastard. Though his mouthing off is usually worse than his bite."

"Motherfucker," Pen spits out.

"I wonder why his mom uprooted Callum and moved to the states?" I ask, since Callum is tight lipped with that bit of detail.

"From what Callum told us when we were kids, Brian was involved in illegal shit with back in Australia, but he didn't know what. And it was Callum's grandfather who sent them here," Danny whispers.

"You ladies talk too damn loud," Callum mutters sleepily. "And that's all hearsay about Australia."

"Sorry," Danny utters.

"Too late. I'm awake. And no, Brian might be a fucker—but I don't see him wanting to physically harm me. In all the years..." Callum yawns... "he's only hit me once. But Granddad put a stop to that. If he had ever laid a hand on me again, Granddad would have skinned him alive with his Bushman."

Callum tries to sit up, but I quickly lay my hand on his chest to stop him. "Hold still," I order. "Let me move the bed into a better position for you." I take the remote from his hand and slowly incline the top half of the bed until Callum winces. "Shit. Let me move it back down a hair."

"No. This is good." Callum smiles, sort of, before shifting his attention to his bandmates. "Why do you two look like crap?"

"Because we've been worried about you, asshole," Danny says with watery eyes. "Who did this to you?"

"I don't know. I didn't get a look at the guy's face."

Callum blows out a heavy breath. "When I opened the door, all I saw was a guy in a hoodie standing there with his back to me. The next thing I knew, I was down on the floor."

"Whover this fucker is, he's a dead man," Connor growls.

"I wouldn't be saying that out loud," Danny grimaces to his bandmate, as he slides more lip gloss across his lips.

"I would agree, since the detectives are on their way here," I remind them. The band seems to be a magnet for trouble, and we don't need to create more.

"Too late, they're already here," Lyric announces as he walks in. "Mr. Fitz, are you up for talking?"

"Please, call me Callum. I'm not my father. And yes, might as well get this over with," he says with a sigh.

"Alright. And I also want to let you know that I'm going off duty," Lyric says before turning to me. "Veronica will be here shortly. She's great. She knows what's going on and the stipulations on who comes in and out of Callum's room."

"I don't like that idea. I told you we want only you to tend to Callum while he's here," I say, not trusting just anyone for Callum's care. Granted, I don't know this male nurse either, but something's telling me that I can trust him. And I always follow my gut.

"I'm sorry, but the hospital made a concession to your request and allowed me to finish my shift up here. And I guarantee you that they won't pay me overtime. So, you'll have to deal with it. Veronica is good and I trust her."

The moment Lyric stops talking, Dante appears in the doorway like a magician. Their makeup is flawless, their suit cut to perfection, and their trademark four-inch black heels don on their feet. Dante's androgynous look belies their Rottweiler tendencies, and right now their eyes are sharp like a knife's edge as they focus unblinkingly on Lyric. "Please, may I have a word with you?"

"Umm... Sure," Lyric says hesitantly and follows the band's manager out of the room.

"What was that all about?" Danny asks, looking at each of us.

"I have no clue," I say before we are interrupted again as Detectives Faller and Longe stride into the room.

They both scan the space before Longe says, "I'm assuming this is the rest of the band?"

"No, only two of five. I'm Danny Wells, and this is Connor Wild." Danny extends his hand, which Faller shakes.

Longe ignores the greeting and moves to the foot of the bed. "If you don't mind stepping out of the room, we have a few questions we want to ask Mr. Fitz." His eyes jump to me, to Pen, and then to Danny and Connor.

"No," I say flatly. "We're on duty and we're not leaving Mr. Fitz."

"Dom," Pen says in warning.

"Mr. Rossetti," Longe begins, but I cut him off.

"We are Mr. Fitz's bodyguards. We will remain here, with him." I narrow my eyes on the cops, giving no fucks if either detective likes it. Pen and I aren't leaving Callum's side.

Tobias and Dante come into the room and I smirk. I can't wait to see the detectives try to go toe-to-toe with the band manager.

Our lead eyes me and then assesses the electricity in the room. "I'll stay with Callum," he jumps in.

"For legality purposes, I have to also," Dante adds, then looks at Detective Longe. "I'm Dante Ross, the band's manager. My pros are they and them."

I watch the detective slow blink as he takes in Dante, then quickly gather himself.

"That's fine," Detective Faller says, not affected one bit with Dante's announcement.

"We're not leaving either," I insist.

Tobias shakes his head. "You two are way too close to this. You and Pen go with the band to the waiting room." His rigid tone gives me no room to argue—no matter how much I detest his interference. But I get it. Pen and I *are* too close to this case—too emotionally connected to be reasonable—especially me.

"Nothing's going to happen to me. Go," Callum says sleepily, but the glazed look in his eyes shows that the drugs to numb his pain still have him feeling slightly high.

"Want to lean back a bit?" Without waiting for his agreement, I grab the controller and lean Callum back a little more. He sighs with relief and the corners of his eyes lose their hard lines.

"Thanks," Callum mumbles out, his shoulders relaxing. My guy isn't going to last long before he falls back to sleep.

I shoot a warning glance at Tobias to keep Callum's comfort in mind before Pen and I leave the room.

"Callum will be okay," Pen says, but there's worry in his words.

"Between the cops, Tobias and me standing guard next to the bed, no one's going in there to hurt him. I promise," Dante says and waves us off.

I don't know what it is, but I'm not comforted by Dante's encouragement. Something in my gut is telling me that Callum's attacker will try again.

Chapter Six

C allum

"It's late and you can stop this at any time, Callum," Dante advises in a whisper. Then they turn to Tobias for confirmation.

Tobias nods. "Dante's right. It's late, so please keep it brief. And understand this, detectives, when Mr. Fitz says stop, it means stop."

Longe looks pointedly at Tobias before focusing his attention on me. "Mr. Fitz, can you tell us what happened earlier today? Can you break it down for us from the time you landed in Colorado?" he asks with a note of authority.

I tell them everything that happened since I arrived at Denver International Airport. All of it uneventful. "I was about to make myself a late lunch, when someone knocked on the door. I opened it and that was when I was attacked. I didn't see the guy's face. And yes, it was a man. I heard his voice."

"Are you sure you didn't see his face—anything—even something small might help," Longe says as he taps things out on his phone.

"No. I don't remember much. The bastard might be about six feet but he was wearing a hoodie and had his back to the door when I opened it. For a split second, when he turned around, I saw he had brown hair—I think... that's all I got. But I have video surveillance on the house. The cameras must have recorded who was at my door," I insist, but both detectives frown.

"Whoever attacked you got to your surveillance room and destroyed all the equipment. Even your storage stacks. They were so damaged our tech guy couldn't retrieve any evidence from them," Faller explains.

"Are you sure?" Tobias asks as he straightens to his full height and eyes the detective. "We have people who are good at that."

"Levi," Dante says with a nod.

"I'm sure you do, but it's confirmed by our team," Faller says before turning his attention to me. "Do you have enemies, Mr. Fitz?" he asks me, his voice gentle. He must be the good cop in this duo.

"No—not really."

"What do you mean not really?" Longe jumps in.

"I mean I don't hang with anyone other than my friends in the band and the security team." Geez, now I sound like a big loser.

"Is that it?" Dante asks, their tone suggesting the interrogation is done.

"One final question," Faller says. "Your security guard,

Dom, told my partner that your attacker said something to you. What was it?"

I swallow hard, thinking back... *Did that prick say anything to me?* "Wait... Yes. He told me something about Brian." I grip the sheet, trying to recall the words. No one utters a word while I search from my memory. Finally, it comes to me. "He said... to tell Brian to stay out of his business or *I'm* going to die the next time." I look at Tobias as my stomach twists. "Yes, that's it. That's what he said."

Longe and Faller glance at each other, then Longe nods. "Brian Fitz is already on our radar," he harumphs. "Mr. Fitz, are you sure that there's no past lover—a woman you could have pissed off, who would come after you?"

"Well, if you're aiming for that, then you're going in the wrong direction. I'm gay," I say flatly.

Now that I think about it, this is the first time I have openly expressed my sexuality to anyone outside my friends and security—I'm mean, it really isn't a big thing. So it can't be that I like men.

There hasn't been any opportunity or reason to, except when I came out to my mother, who was happy for me. But my father... When Brian overheard my confession, it hadn't boded well. Thankfully, his opinion didn't matter then... Or now.

"Then no male ex-lovers?" Longe asks like he has chalk dust in his mouth.

Since my best friends are gay... Okay, I'm not so sure about Bobby. "Nobody comes to mind."

"Good to know," Faller says smoothly, and there's a hint of smile across his handsome face.

I have to admit that Detective Faller is exactly my type. He's tall, has a level of charm I'm suddenly seeing, and there's a twinkle in his light blue eyes that's aimed at me... My breath hitches and warmth seeps into my blood.

Then I realize that the desire in his eyes doesn't make me nearly as hot as when Dom and Pen look at me with the same intensity Faller's conveying. Their smolder makes my blood hum, my dick rock hard and my balls ache to be touched.

Tobias clears his throat. He narrows his eyes on Faller. "Are we done here?" His words are sharp and his tone is a demand.

Faller's back snaps straight and he quickly fixes his black tie. "No stalker?"

"No, that would be Danny," I respond immediately, then glance at Tobias, who's smirking.

"No family members—aside from your father, that you suspect?" Longe throws in.

"No. That would be Connor," I reply, cracking a small smile.

A deep groove forms between Faller's and Longe's brows. "Explain," they say in unison.

"You don't have to answer that. It's not pertinent to what's happening now," Dante says, folding their arms across their chest.

I glance at them, and then sheepishly add, "Both are long, boring stories."

Longe raises a finger. "Quick question and then we'll get out of your hair. Why do you call your father by his first name?"

"You don't have to answer that either—Detectives, please! Stick to the case in hand." Dante glares at them.

"It's okay, Dante." I inhale, and continue. "Actually, Brian is his middle name and he has always used it as his first for as long as I can remember. I go by my first name, even though unfortunately I'm a junior."

"Okay, but why Brian?" Longe insists.

"I call him Brian because he's not deserving of the title of father. You have to be loving, good to your wife and cherish your child. He hasn't done that on any level."

"That's it?" Longe says before sliding his phone back into his pocket.

"It's that simple," I admit with honesty. I don't know what Longe wanted me to say.

"There's nothing simple, especially in this case." Longe shakes his head. "Do you think your father is involved in your attack?"

"I wouldn't put it past him," I look away, feeling embarrassed that the man that gave me life is a total jack-hole.

"Okay," Faller says. "We will keep in touch. And here," he passes a card to me, but Dante takes it from the detective's fingers. "If you have any questions, you can reach us at this number."

With a parting nod, both detectives leave my room.

"Do you actually think your father had something to do with your assault?" Dante asks, a note of anger lacing their voice.

"It's the only valid thing I can think of." I slump against the pillow and sigh.

Tobias pinches the bridge of his nose before he looks at me. "I'm sorry to say this, but my number one priority is to make sure you and the rest of the band are safe. Your father will not ever be permitted anywhere that you and the band are. Understand, Callum?"

"I get it. He's trouble."

"Dean is looking into your father's current and past dealings. Would that be okay with you?" Dante asks—but why ask me, knowing they already started investigating Brian?

"I don't have a problem with that, but my concern is for

my mother. I have a feeling she might be unintentionally mixed up in this too—Oh God," I gasp.

"What?" Tobias asks.

"My mother. I need to call her." I jolt up right, and pain suddenly tears through my body. "She might be the next target—fuck, I need to call her," I say as panic weighs heavy in my chest.

Tobias grips my shoulder gently. "Then we'll get someone on her immediately, I promise, Callum. In the meantime, we need you to rest."

"I have to tell Pen and Dom."

Dante leans in. "You need to calm yourself, Callum. Tobias and the team will handle this and your mother will be safe."

Tobias straightens and eyes Dante. "I don't want the band to know what's going down—not yet anyway. Because you know what will happen if Danny finds out."

Dante slowly nods. "Danny will go ballistic. He'll try to track down Brian and more chaos will ensue."

"Yes," Tobias breathes out.

"I need to call my mother," I demand, as I fight off Tobias's grip on shoulder. "Tobias—damn it."

"You need to calm down first," Dante says firmly. "Here, use my phone."

"Callum, look at me. We don't want to alarm your mother in case nothing is happening with her. But if she doesn't answer, then I'll call Dean and he'll get someone to her right away. Okay?"

I stop fighting his hold. "Alright." Then I grab Dante's phone and call my mother.

She answers in two rings, and her sweet melodic voice eases the pressure in my chest and I begin to tear up. "Mum?"

"Hey, my boy."

Her calm endearment alleviates my worry as I begin telling her what happened to me.

Chapter Seven

P en

As I pace the waiting room, Detective Faller walks in and goes straight to Dom. I'm glad it's him and not his callous partner.

"Mr. Rossetti, Mr. Gallagher, I just want to reiterate that if you remember anything from today, I don't care how minor the detail might seem, call me," he says evenly.

"Do you have any leads?" Dom asks, his body taut like he would break in half if I touched him. So I keep the little distance I have between him and me.

"There might be something, but Longe and I are working on that."

"There's only one person," Danny chimes in as he straightens in his seat and a sneer slides into place. "Brian Fitz."

"He's on the list," Faller admits, then turns back to us. "Like I said, think of anything, let me know." He glances around the room, smirks and then leaves.

"Did everyone see that?" Bobby asks as he unwraps a new sucker and sticks it into his mouth. If the band's keyboardist keeps up with the sugar, his mouth will be full of cavities.

"Yeah, I've seen that look before," Rafe says, scratching at his scruffy jaw. "Appreciation."

"Maybe he knows who we are and likes our music," Danny adds with a half-cocked grin.

"No, Rafe's right," Connor weighs in. "Appreciation of eye candy. And we are a handsome bunch." The drummer chortles while his hands air drum to an imaginary beat.

"Babe." John slides his hand around the back of his lover's neck and squeezes. "Behave."

"What?" Connor asks in mock innocence. "I'm only speaking truth. We're hella hot."

Soft chuckles echo around the room before quiet descends upon the space again, as we each reflect on the true reason why we're here. Callum.

Then Tobias walks into the room, with Dante right behind him, and announces, "Callum's asleep."

"And you two left him alone?" Dom hisses as he takes a step toward the door.

Tobias's eyes sharpen on Dom's face. "No. The nurse is with him."

Dom's shoulder relaxes. "Sorry. It's just that..."

"I know," Tobias says knowingly, which confuses me. Does he know Dom and I have feelings for Callum? Does he know about the three of us?

"Do you really think Callum's dad is involved in this attack?" Connor asks as he leans into his boyfriend.

"Anything is possible," John says, squeezing the drummer's hand.

Bobby drops down next to Rafe and looks at the lead guitarist. "I didn't get enough sleep in Vegas."

Rafe smirks. "Sleep? What sleep? I was at that damn poker table all night. I'm surprised I had enough energy to get to the condo before we got the call."

"I ran out of money long before you," Bobby gripes and looks away, pulling the sucker out of his mouth with a pop.

I glance over at Dom, who remains quiet but is staring at John and Tobias. It's like they are communicating without using their mouths. I don't know how those three do that, but it still boggles my mind. I tried it myself once, attempting to convey what I was thinking to Dom by focusing my gaze on him. Then once with Fig—Bobby's security guy, who's currently roaming the hallways of the hospital. But each time was a wasted effort on my part.

My phone rings, and not a second later, so does Dom's. I pull mine out and glance at my screen. My stomach bottoms out, seeing the name displayed. It's my mother, Margaret Gallagher—Margie to her close friends and family.

I didn't come out to my parents until the summer we went to Rocktoberfest for the first time. Before that, there hadn't been a reason—every guy I'd been with was just a hookup. So I put it off as long as I could, knowing exactly how they'd react—and I was right.

My family practically excommunicated me. Ron says waiting was the smart move; otherwise, I'd have faced all that hatred way too young. But after I met Dom, and genuine feelings started to develop, and staying quiet wasn't an option anymore. I had to tell my parents.

Still, it's been kind of weird lately. In the last four months, my mother has been calling me. The first time, I was elated to hear from her, until I realized she'd gotten it into her head that she needed to talk me out of my *lifestyle*—her words.

Each call follows the same script: her reasons and God's path. She says she wants to *understand me*, but the words she ends up using make it seem more like she's praying the gay away. And I reply that God has nothing to do with my sexuality and not to call me again unless she wants to talk about other things in my life. Like my music. The guys. Anything else other than who I'd prefer as my bed partner.

Ron says that I'm lucky that my mother wants to talk. But I don't have to endure her verbal diatribe. Therefore, I stopped answering her calls.

Today's call is her sixth this week. Despite all their homophobia and religious zeal, I still love my parents and miss them—or rather, the *them* I knew before I came out, but I can't make myself a target any more.

I stifle a groan as I decline the call and shove my phone back in my pocket. Can you imagine what it'd be like if they found out about my relationship with Dom, and our hope that Callum joins us? No. I vow that will never happen—they'll never know.

Sighing, I glance at Dom, whose face reflects a mild confusion. No one from the band notices the shift in tension, but I can see the way our security team are each poised stoically still, every pair of eyes trained on my man.

I walk over to him and quietly ask, "What's wrong?" Dom meets my eyes and after a barely perceptible shake of his head, I shut my mouth. *Later*, I think he's silently conveying to me. *Wow—this silent message thing works!*

Without another word, Dom leaves the waiting room, and I quickly follow. He whirls around and growls, "I need a moment, Pen." Without a parting glance, he heads to the elevator and presses the down button.

"What the hell?" I mutter to myself.

"What did he say?" Tobias reaches my side, his eyes focused on Dom and the closing elevator door.

"He didn't tell me anything. Just that he needs a moment," I reply, feeling slightly gut-punched by Dom's dismissive attitude and abrupt departure.

"Whatever it is, the message he got had to be bad news," Tobias says evenly.

My lead is right. It has to be something monumental, if Dom's leaving without telling me or checking on Callum. But I can't imagine what it is. I hate it when Dom keeps things from me. And lately that seems to be happening more than I like.

"I'm going to sit with Callum." I finally turn my attention away from the elevator, hoping that I'll soon find out what his text message was all about.

"I'll have Fig stay as your back up. Now I need to find Dante. I'm curious about what they had to say to Lyric."

"I have no clue," I admit and walk down the hall to Callum's room.

My brain runs through possible reasons why Dom left so suddenly and why the band manager is nowhere in sight, and come up with nothing. But I've always been a patient man— my mom used to tell me *Your patience is your fortune.*

That memory brings me up short, as regret and sorrow filter in, blotting out my confidence, all because of one little word. *Gay.* I was gay for all the years they loved me, and I'm still me.

Jesus, I'm such a cliché. Inwardly complaining that my family doesn't want anything to do with me while I should be thankful for my found family—the people who do care for me, and my job.

And Dom? After tonight, and the way he's been keeping things from me, I'm not as sure about our relationship any more.

I sit with Callum, who's in and out of sleep with the drugs in his system. I keep checking my phone but my messages to Dom go unanswered. Now it's hitting the six-hour mark since he left, and Dom's lack of contact has made my patience fly out the window.

Chapter Eight

D^{om}

The strange SOS text from Rick Morrison, my old partner from when I was a U.S. Marshal, shocks me. The last time I talked to him was over ten years ago, after all the shit that went down years ago. Now, out of the blue, he texts me to get my ass to his place in Chicago before someone kills him? Hell, I didn't even know he moved from Virginia to the windy city.

I'm thrown back into the clusterfuck of that day fourteen years ago. It ended my career and left me with a brutal scar, but Rick lost so much more. His wife left him—taking his only child with her, while he was still in the hospital recovering from gun shots he took to his chest and right arm. He'd been a dependable partner and he'd saved my life that day, so I owe him.

Knowing Callum is in good hands, and Pen and the rest of the security team are protecting him, I have no worries about leaving. And the sooner I get going, the faster I get back to them.

I call Dean and ask to borrow his jet, then call Tobias and tell him what's going down. I should tell Pen, too, because keeping him in the dark is a shitty thing to do. But when it comes to personal shit, he overthinks and over analyzes everything. Once I find out what Rick needs from me, then I'll tell Pen what's going on. And I'll tell him about my past, too, when I get back.

While en route to Chicago, I get several text messages from Pen. The guilt is eating at me, especially when I replay the moment I barked at him to back off. I should have told him about my past right then so he'd understand that I have to go to Rick, but something stopped me.

Besides, with Callum's attack and the assailant still free, Pen has enough to worry about. It wasn't the right time to explain who I used to be. Or that's the excuse I cling to.

Once I get off the plane at Midway Airport, I'm met by Jaeger, another one of Dean's guys, who has a rental car waiting for me. I tap the address Rick texted me into the GPS, then head south on Route 50 toward Chicago Heights.

Jaeger warned me that Rick's place is in a less-than-reputable area of the city and I need to be on guard. But I'm not worried. I pull up to a three-flat on South Peoria and park right out front of the three flat.

Before unfolding myself out of the rental, I pat my side, making sure my Beretta's there.

Staring up at the third floor, I lock the car and proceed to climb the two flights of stairs until I'm standing in front of Rick's door.

Glancing at the keycode mechanism on the door, I punch in the five numbers Rick texted me while I was driving here. With a soft snick, the lock opens and I push the door ajar.

I listen, but there's no noise. "Rick," I call out softly and open the door an inch wider. Still no noise.

When my ears catch a click, I withdraw my gun and use my foot to widen the gap of the door until I'm able to see a good portion of the living area and kitchenette—both trashed up with liquor bottles, beer cans and takeout containers.

"Rick, it's Dom," I call out louder this time, still keeping most of my body in the hallway.

"Dominic?" A cracked voice sounds off from the other end of the apartment.

I push the door all the way open and see my old partner peeking around a doorway, with a gun in his hand aimed at me.

"It's me," I say, keeping my eyes on Rick and his unsteady hand. "Are you going to lower your gun or are we going to have a problem?"

Relief slides across his face as he lowers the gun. "It's good to see you, man. Come in." He scratches his fingernails through the top of his buzz cut as he shuffles his way to the gray sofa in the living area.

I slip my gun back in its holster by my ribs, then cautiously enter the apartment and close the door behind me. I take a real good look around the place and it's a total pigsty. He doesn't look so great, either. But I keep my opinion to myself. If the man has issues cleaning up his place and himself, it's not up to me to tell him so.

"I'm here, Rick. Now what's the SOS?" I ask, my attention back on my ex-partner, and taking in his disheveled state.

He nods, "Yeah. Get to the point, idiot," he mutters to

himself before focusing his bloodshot eyes on me. "Someone is after me," he says as he grabs an open cigarette pack and snags one. He lights it with a shaky hand before planting himself on the sofa. He takes a large drag of the cigarette and blows smoke out.

"Explain," I say, not bothering to sit since there's so much shit piled on top of the only chair in the room and I was *not* joining him on the dirty sofa.

"Last week, I was walking through the grocery store and I saw a guy following me. I didn't think anything of it at the time until earlier today when I was coming back from getting cigarettes and happened to look over to the other side of the street. It was the same guy, Dom—I swear it."

"And?"

"I kept on walking, but the bastard crept up from behind and hit me in the back of the head and then took off." Rick stands, smashes the cigarette into some dried up food still in a takeout box on the coffee table, then turns around and points to a lump large enough for me to see from where I'm standing. "By the time I got up from the ground the fucker was gone."

"Did you call the cops?"

Rick spins back around and glares at me. "Have you seen my neighborhood? The cops rarely cruise around here. And no, they wouldn't do a fucking thing. I'll handle it myself."

I narrow my gaze on him. He's twitchy, like he's coming down from a high. "Then why text me and have me come all this way? Jesus, Rick, did you drunk text me?"

"No—No. I..." He reaches for another cigarette. "I don't think my attack was random."

My body goes stiff at his words. "What do you mean?"

"I mean someone is out to hurt me—or worse, kill me. I

know I've been out of the game for a while, but I know when I'm being watched."

Out of all the things he could say, that's the one that grabs me. Then I think of Callum... No way these two attacks are related.

Furthermore, the way Rick is acting... Suspect. He's manic and tweaking from the lack of drugs in his system. I hate to think my old friend is battling a drug and alcohol problem, but the proof is all around the apartment. Crumpled up and blackened aluminum foil and empty beer cans and alcohol are strewn about the place.

At first, I thought he might be delusional, but the large bump on the back of his head says otherwise.

"How about this? I have a friend who has a private security agency here. I trust him. Let me call him and see what he can do."

"I don't have the money for that shit, Dominic. After they released me from the hospital, our asshole boss put me on fucking desk duty. I didn't last a year man," Rick cries, wiping his runny nose with the back of his hand.

But that was fourteen years ago. I keep that part to myself, though, because where would I be now without Dean?

"I'm on disability. I don't make jack shit. After Noelle left me, I wasn't able to get back to my normal. It's that bitch's fault. She won't even let me see my own son. But you know what, I have my ways. Want to see what Joshy looks like now? He's a freshman at Cornell." He pulls out his phone, taps it a few times and then hands it to me. "See?"

The first thing I notice is the broken screen. Then I focus on the photo. The image is grainy at best, probably because it was taken from afar. But it's enough to see the boy's face. "I'm sure he's happy to see you now."

"No. Noelle took out a restraining order. No less than five hundred feet. That bitch. If you make a family, make sure your partner doesn't take your fucking kid away man."

I pass him back his phone and clear my throat. The weight of our past isn't as heavy a burden to me as it is to Rick, which seals my commitment to help him. All this time, he's been stuck in this perpetual cycle of near insanity, while I got out because Dean pulled me out.

If it wasn't for my longtime friendship with Dean Harper —meeting him during my short stint in the military, I don't know where I'd be right now. *Maybe like Rick.*

"I need your help, Dom," Rick says as he stubs out the half-smoked cigarette, then grabs for another.

"I'm not sure what I can do, but…" I think for a second, remembering a friend of mine that moved back to Chicago. "I have a friend who might help. I'm going to call Leo and give him the details—you don't mind if I give him your number?"

Rick shakes his head, puffing out a plume of smoke through his nose. "No, man. I'd appreciate it."

"Leo owes me a favor. Just give him the details, and then we can go from there. Alright?" I ask, not sure what else to do for him. If anyone can get the answers, it's Leo Richards.

"I don't know what to say." Rick stands and extends his hand. I glance down at it and for a second, I notice how clean his fingernails are. "Thanks, man," he says graciously, which pulls my focus.

I grip his hand and shake it. Then releasing him, I slowly move to the door. "Rick."

His watery, bloodshot eyes meet mine. "Yeah?"

"Watch your surroundings. And take care of yourself. I'll be in touch."

He drops down onto the sofa and blows out a long breath of smoke. "I will."

Something about his response niggles at me as I close the door of his apartment and head to my rental car. The entire ride back to the airport, my mind keeps wondering—if Dean hadn't pulled me out of the pit of hell and straightened my ass out, would I have turned out to be like Rick?

Chapter Nine

C allum

Since the head nurse told everyone to leave about an hour ago, I've been sitting here, eyes wide open, not able to sleep.

I pick up my cell phone and see that it's nearly ten p.m. I send Pen a text, telling him I'm okay.

When the nurse kicked them out, Tobias insisted that Pen go too. I don't like the idea of being left here without Pen or Dom, but I understand why Tobias commanded Pen to go. He wouldn't do anyone—especially me, any good if he's dead on his feet. Tobias assured me that Fig will be close by, while Pen gets some rest for a few hours.

Pen wasn't happy about the order. Actually, he wasn't happy the last few hours. Although, I was too tired from the pain meds to push to ask him why he was in a grouchy state.

Especially after Danny and the guys explained that Dom abruptly left without a word to anyone.

So where's Dom?

I asked Tobias, but he refused to answer me, and I didn't push him either.

I unclip the oxygen sensor from my finger and then carefully lean over, working around the damn IV lines, and grab the neck of the acoustic guitar with my uninjured hand.

When Danny walked into my room earlier with it, I almost cried. In the middle of all the chaos, he had gone to the house and brought me my guitar and stand—one of my most prized possessions. It had belonged to my granddad, who used to call it his *banjo*, and I had always loved watching him play.

Before Tobias made everyone leave, he had Rafe set it in the guitar stand he'd put beside my bed.

I manage to get the guitar situated on my lap, but then I have to wiggle it a bit so the fingers of my splinted left arm can reach the fretboard. Fortunately, the splint they gave me only covers my arm from my elbow to my wrist, otherwise this would be impossible. I try a few test strums—considering my soreness, the wires, and my splint, I'm not playing with finesse.

Still, every strum of a chord is such a sweet and simple sound that it evokes another set of aches—ones tied to emotions I've buried deep down that are fighting to rise to the surface. While I'm not ready to face them yet, the music still lightens my mood. I don't feel as glum as I did even though I'm still sitting in a hospital bed alone.

I lightly strum my fingers across the strings, and remember the day Granddad gave the guitar to me. It was the day before my mum and I left for the states. I was ten—almost eleven at the time, and I never thought back then that it would be the last time I'd see that old man ever again. To this day, I miss the gruff bastard.

I begin playing the first song I learned on this guitar. Granddad taught it to me while we were on one of our camping trips out in the Bush. It starts off soft, and as I rack my memory for the lyrics, I try whispering the words.

So focused on what I'm playing, I don't see Lyric standing in the doorway listening until the end of the song. Then I hear him walk inside the room and close the door.

"Hey wait a minute. I thought you were off duty a couple hours ago."

"Yes, I was until another nurse called in sick. And since I was already here, the hospital authorized the double shift for me."

"That sucks."

"Meh. We are short staffed, but I will love the paycheck. Anyway, I'm the only one who doesn't have family or a pet at home, so why not." Lyric shrugs and then takes a seat next to the bed.

"Still sucks," I echo my sentiment. "So you'll be taking care of me instead of Veronica?"

"You have two for the price of one." He winks. "Now enough about me. What's the song about? It's beautiful but sad."

"It's called The Dying Stockman—it's an old Bush song. My granddad taught it to me when I was a kid."

"Now that's kind of cool to learn something so old," he says with a smile and I can see the charming person behind his strict nursing persona.

"If my granddad heard that, he'd wrap his knuckles on top of your head and declare he wasn't old." I laugh, and so does Lyric.

"Hey, do you want me to call your grandfather for you?

I'm sure he'd be happy to hear from you." Lyric stands, but I shake my head.

"No. Sadly, he died seventeen years ago. But I miss him every day," I admit, my heart aching at the loss all over again. Needing to change the subject before I end up crying like a baby, I ask, "What did Dante want to talk to you about?"

"Umm..." Lyric looks away. Wait. Is that a blush across his cheeks?

"Are you blushing?"

"No," Lyric protests in a whisper. "I don't know if I should say anything now. It's not official yet."

"Official? Hmm. Now you have to tell me," I push, hoping he spills the secret.

Lyric leans in, a smile splitting his pretty face. "Dante wants to hire me."

"For what?"

"As a full-time caregiver—Dante's words." Lyric chuckles. "They made it sound like I'm going to take care of toddlers."

"Some of us do act like it at times," I say with a laugh, then wince from the pain. "Laughing makes my face hurt."

"Then stop." Lyric giggles again. "I assume Dante wants to hire me to tend to you, but you seem like you're doing good. So I asked them who I would be taking care of, and they said I'll be available for the band," he explains with a shrug. "Something about you boys get into way too much shit. But I'm still waiting on Dante to call me back—they need to get the okay from the record label."

"Are you considering it?"

Lyric's questioning gaze meets mine. "I'm still thinking about the offer. It's a commitment."

"It is," I say earnestly.

"What kind of situations does your band get into that would need a medical personnel member on the tour?"

"You'd be surprised." I stop to think about all the craziness that has happened in the past couple of years, and have to admit, "Maybe Dante's right." I strum my fingers across the strings, smiling.

"Anyway," Lyric stands. "The real reason I came in here is that, even though I love hearing you play, the patient next door doesn't. Mr. Dillon requests that you stop playing and go to sleep." He wrinkles his nose and has a growly tone to his voice, mimicking a grouchy old man.

I chuckle. "Got it." I ask Lyric to place the guitar in the stand and move it away from the bed. "Thanks."

"No prob. If you need anything, I'm right outside." With that, Lyric leaves.

I recline my bed, settle in and quickly fall asleep. But just as fleetingly, my nightmares begin to assault me and I'm being attacked. Fists punch my face. Boots kick my torso—I try to curl up in a ball, but the attack keeps coming.

A scream is lodged in my throat, and my entire body is shaking.

"Wake up, sweetheart. It's Dom. Wake up."

I blink several times before the frenzy of my rapidly beating heart calms and my eyes settle on Dom's handsome, rugged face. "Dom?"

"It's okay. I'm here," Dom says in a soothing tone I haven't heard him use before.

"I was being at—" I utter shakily.

"It was a dream, I'm here now," he whispers hoarsely.

Still shaky, I reach for his hand. "Please don't leave."

"I'm not going anywhere."

"Lay with me?" I plead, and grip his hand tighter.

"Are you sure I won't hurt you by laying down next to you?"

"No." I gingerly move over, making room so Dom can climb into the bed. I'd gladly give up the majority of the space to feel his body against mine. To feel the solace his touch gives me. Anything to keep from sinking back into the nightmare in my head.

"As long as you're okay. I don't want Lyric coming in here and chasing me out." Dom settles on his side, before he cups my face. His touch soothes away the panic and eases my racing heart.

"Where did you go?" I ask while nuzzling my face against his chest, but my entire body still trembles.

"I went to help an old friend I used to work with." He draws me closer to his body and I appreciate his warmth and his solid presence.

The solemnity of what he said has me questioning why this was such a big deal for Pen. "That's it? No other explanation?" I question.

"What do you want me to say?" He pulls back, and I see his brows furrow into a deep crease.

"I don't know... Maybe try giving a better explanation for why you ghosted Pen and left him in the dark about where you went?" I can't hide the small irritation. He's acting like what he did was no big deal — but it *was* for Pen. Why? "Pen's upset. You need to talk to him."

"I know." His arms tighten even more around me. "And I'll fix it tomorrow. Promise."

"It is tomorrow," I frown, then groan from the slight pain shooting across my face. "You better do it soon because I hate seeing him looking like someone kicked his puppy."

Dom chuckles.

"It's not funny." I jab a finger in his chest.

He loosens his hold a bit. "I'm sorry, and yeah, it's not funny. I will talk to Pen when he gets here. But someone kicked his puppy?"

I poke him again. "Again, not funny."

He kisses my temple. "You're right."

I meet Dom's eyes—those dark brown depths hold a wealth of secrets. But I don't push. "Good." I'm not normally a touchy-feely kind of man, but in this moment—especially after waking up from a nightmare, Dom lying beside me feels good, like this is our normal. Like we have a life where there's no contempt or pressure from people around us. Including any pressures we might put on each other.

Just because I'm enjoying this now doesn't mean that Dom, Pen and I are going to be together. Sleeping with them doesn't mean I want a commitment. And Dom holding me doesn't mean we're together either.

"Speaking of Pen, why isn't he here? I told him not to leave your side," he rumbles out.

"Tobias ordered him to go shower, eat and rest for a bit before coming back. It's okay, Dom. Fig's roaming the halls and checking in to see if I'm okay. I've been texting him."

"No, it's not okay. I texted Tobias that Pen needs to stay. I didn't want you to be alone."

"He's not."

We both swivel our heads to the doorway and I see Fig standing in the threshold, wearing a set of scrubs that looks a size too small. The smirk on his face conveys nothing about this man.

"Why are you dressed like that?" Dom asks. I'm not able to hide my humor.

Fig's a big guy—way over six feet tall and the scrubs are tight against his bulky frame, making it look as if his muscles are going to burst through the seams any moment.

"Tobias didn't want anyone to know that I'm here watching over Callum. So, I'm incognito, just in case that bastard comes around. What do you think? I look good as a doctor, right? Oh, that male nurse knows I'm here too. He's the one who gave me these scrubs. But he's the only one who knows. Now, I'm going to make my rounds." Fig gives us a small salute and then leaves, closing the door behind him.

"But you're not a doctor," I call out, chuckling.

Dom rolls his eyes. "He's a strange motherfucker."

"Yeah, he is. But I like him."

Dom lets out a grunt of displeasure. "I don't think so."

I slowly shake my head. "You're ridiculous." But inwardly, I smile at how possessive Dom can be.

"I need to call Pen." He tries to get out of the bed, but I gently grip his forearm. "Stop. It's three in the morning, Dom," I say through a yawn. "And I'm tired and want to sleep."

But I'm afraid to close my eyes. Afraid I'd fall back into my nightmare.

Dom gently caresses my face and lays his head down next to mine. "Then go to sleep." he whispers in my ear. His voice is low and gravelly, and the heat his body exudes has me feeling warm, but I still can't rest. I'm more edgy than tired now.

"I'm... afraid to close my eyes," I admit, feeling more out of sorts.

But the moment Dom gently kisses the back of my neck, a frisson of want begins to pool in my belly. "Want me to help you sleep?" Dom trails his hand down my chest until it rests on my stomach.

Is Dom taunting me? Does he know he's turning me on with those annoying kisses and touches? He knows damn well I can't resist him, especially when he's touching me.

"I don't know what you can do." Actually, I know what I want him to do, but I doubt Dom will touch me. Not when I'm injured. Besides, we're in the hospital, and anyone—especially a nurse, could walk in here and see him give me—

"I know what you're thinking, and no."

"Why?" I pout, but my lips hurt and quickly relax my mouth.

"There's no room to maneuver ourselves. And you're hurt and I don't—"

"I'm not asking for much, Dom. Come on. Please touch me," I plead, holding my breath for a moment, waiting on what he's going to say, and I don't have to wait long.

Dom's hand slides under the sheet that covers me, then under the gown I'm wearing. His hand snakes inside my underwear and cups my semi hard cock. "If I do this, you have to be quiet."

"What?" I'm surprise that he would touch me.

"I said yes, but you need to be quiet."

"Okay," I rush to say, as the sensation of want grows in my groin and heat blooms across my body.

"Promise to not utter a word—not a sound, Callum. Promise you're going to relax and let me take care of you," he whispers.

I nod, not uttering a word.

Dom carefully climbs off the bed, and I want to protest until he pulls out his wallet and takes out a small packet. He then goes into the bathroom and returns with a washcloth.

I peer into his hand. "Lube?"

"Never leave home without it," he says with a wicked grin and climbs back into the bed with me. "Now hush."

Dom uncovers me, exposing my stomach, part of my chest and my straining cock. He tucks my balls over the band of my underwear, the pressure heightening the pleasure.

He drops the washcloth on my belly and says, "Can't have Lyric finding my man's gown glued to his stomach with dried up spunk."

My man. I am equal parts terrified and elated.

With a wicked smile, Dom rips open the packet and dribbles the lube into his hand, then wraps his fingers around my hard length and strokes.

I silently groan, closing my eyes, and the sensation of his firm grip on my cock has me flying high, desperate to come. But it isn't enough. Instead of telling him, I move my hips in rhythm, both in pleasure and pain.

"Greedy," he whispers in my ear, and I shiver at the feather touch of his breath along my skin. His hand speeds up. Up and down in quick hard pumps until my hips meet up with his downward grip. "Next time, I'll draw this out. Make you wait until your balls ache and your cockhead is dribbling with precum. Slowly suck up your flavor, work your cock to the point you're ready to blow. Then I will stop and do it all over again... while Pen watches as he strokes his own dick. Would you like that, sweetheart?"

Fuck... yes... Dominic, I think as sparks explode across my vision and I fall over the edge. Dom doesn't stop stroking my dick until he milks every last bit of my seed out of my balls.

"That's it, baby. Give me everything you have. I'm hungry for a taste again."

I watch Dom's face as he pulls his hand from below my dick and licks my cum from his fingers. My cock twitches at the sight, but I'm way too drained for more. I close my eyes, feeling loopy and totally exhausted. I don't protest when he wipes me clean.

"Now get some sleep." The soothing tone of Dom's voice has me sinking deeper into sleep, knowing I'm safe.

Chapter Ten

P en

A shower and a few hours of sleep do nothing to assuage the guilt I feel about leaving Callum alone at the hospital. Even though Fig promised to text me updates while he's patrolling, and even though I find a few texts from Callum when I wake up that each let me know he's fine, being away from Callum just doesn't feel right.

I'm also feeling annoyed and unwanted because I still haven't heard a word from Dom.

Against Tobias's order to wait for him and the rest of the team to go back to the hospital together, I take one of the SUVs and leave by myself.

Visiting hours don't start until seven, but I don't give a shit. It's just after six in the morning when I file out of the elevator onto the third floor and stride down the hall toward

Callum's room. I'm determined to land my eyes on the man and make sure he's okay and safe. Nothing on Fig, and it's not that I don't trust him to protect Callum, but Callum's *my* responsibility to protect.

The nurse's station is empty. I figure whoever's working is making their rounds. The second I step inside Callum's room, I freeze. In the bed, Callum is all bundled up in Dom's arms. Both of them are sleeping like they don't have a care in the world.

I take the moment to study the two men that occupy my every thought. Such a contrast. Dom is big and broody, with short, dark wavy hair and an olive skin tone hinting at his Italian heritage.

Callum, with his longish blond hair and California tanned complexion, reminds me of a surfer. The light sprinkle of freckles across the bridge of his nose elevates his attractiveness.

I chuckle seeing them both crammed into the bed. Callum's shy an inch to my five-eleven, and Dom's six-two.

Light to dark, they are *my* yin to *my* yang. I can finally breathe easier now that I know they're together and I'm close to them.

"Are you going to just stand there all morning and stare at us?" Dom grumps, tilting his head enough to side-eye me. I don't know what it is, but morning Dom's sleep-gruff voice always gives me a shot of lust, and today is no different. My dick perks up.

"That all depends," I whisper, walking over to the bed and smiling down at them.

"On what?" His narrowed eyes meet mine with such intensity that prickles of both unease and excitement ripple across my skin in response to his full attention.

Assuming that he at least *read* my texts, Dom knows I'm

upset that he left me without a word. The spark in Dom's eyes shows that *he* is upset that I disobeyed his order to stay with Callum, even though I did it under duress. I've no doubt there will be repercussions coming my way. *And oh God, I hope so.*

"Are you going to give me shit for leaving Callum?" I ask, remaining a few feet from the bed.

"Depends," he says, evenly. "Did Tobias order you to go?" The depth of his tone conveys further warning, but I'm right. Dom being a *dom* is a salacious thing to be around.

"Yes, and I refused but it was no use," I say truthfully.

Dom slowly sits up and a small smirk spreads across his face, making him look a lot younger than his forty years. "Did he twist your—"

The door swings open and a woman walks in, her face partially covered by a mask. Her eyes widen in surprise at seeing us. "I'm here to take Mr. Fitz's vitals," she says with hesitation.

She's unfamiliar to me, but she is wearing the standard dark blue scrubs with the hospital logo on the shirt. Her red hair is in high bun with long ornamental chopsticks sticking out of the mass.

She looks out of place.

She hesitates for moment, assessing Dom and Callum, then me. But her stillness has me on instant alert.

"Where's Lyric?" Dom asks, slowly getting up from the bed, his attention never leaving her face.

The nurse takes two steps, and then everything happens fast. She pulls a gun from behind her back. "Silencer," I shout and move without thought.

Her aim is directed at the two men I care most about. Right as Dom covers Callum with his body, she whirls around and takes a shot at me. The sting doesn't stop me from catapulting myself at her.

On impact, her hand releases the gun and it clatters to the floor. I wrestle her until she's face down, then manage to get her forearms under my knees, and my hand clamped onto the back of her neck. For a small, thin woman, she has strength and nearly gets away from my hold.

"Don't fucking move," I hiss and tighten my hand on the back of her neck, pushing her face into the floor.

"Get off me, asshole. You're hurting me," she screeches.

I ignore her, and ask Callum and Dom without looking at them, "Are you two okay?"

"We're good. But you... You're shot."

"It's only a graze," I say, as the shooter tries to wiggle out of my hold again. I put my full weight into my hold. "Stay fucking still."

Dom climbs off Callum then snatches the gun from the floor and tucks it behind his back as he walks over to me.

"What the hell?" Fig shouts, storming into the room. He then sees me on the ground with the woman. "God-mother-fucking-damn-it!"

"She tried to kill Dom and Callum," I growl.

He rushes to my side, snags her left arm from under my knee, and twists it behind her back. "I got her."

With Fig restraining her, I get up and together we pull the woman onto her feet. Even with both of us holding her, she still tries to kick her way free.

"Stop moving. You're going to hurt yourself," Fig sighs like he's bored.

Dom approaches her, his eyes emanating rage. "Who are you?"

"Fuck you," she spits, trying to get out of our hold. "Fuck you all."

"I suggest you stop fighting, because you're going nowhere," I growl and tighten my hold on her arm.

"Fuck off," she screams this time. "I have rights."

"What the heck is going on?" A female nurse rushes in, her eyes wide with shock.

"Call the police. We just apprehended a shooter who tried to kill me and Mr. Fitz," Dom barks out.

The nurse looks at me, sees the bloody patch on my shirt and then races out of the room.

"Are you going to be okay?" Dom asks me, as he stares at the red spot on my shirt.

"Yeah," I say, waving off the ache in my arm. "I said it's only a graze."

"Let me go, you fucking bastards," she screeches and thrashes against us, putting all her weight into the action before the bitch tries kicking at us again.

Dom moves to me. "I got her." He takes ahold of her arm just above my hands and nods at me to let go; Fig remains firm with his grip and I step back, assessing my arm.

Security shows up right then, but it's a little late. The cops arrive five minutes later, and immediately handcuff the would-be assassin. They cart her away just as Faller and Longe enter the room, along with Tobias and Danny rushing in behind them.

"I told you both to wait outside," Longe grates out, pointing to the doorway.

"Like hell I am," Danny sneers as he hurries to Callum's side and takes his friend's hand. "What the heck, Callum? Are you alright?"

"Yes, I'm fine. It's Pen who's shot." Callum admits, worry creasing the corners of his eyes as they meet mine.

"Go get that checked," Tobias orders as he points to my arm, then he turns to Dom for answers.

"It's only a flesh wound. I'm fine," I insist, as Rafe, Bobby, Connor and John enter. *Christ, we're packed in here like sardines.*

"Pen," Dom snaps, glaring at me before returning his attention to our lead.

"Jesus—fine." I give in, even though I don't want to leave the room.

"I'll get the gist from Pen," John says as Connor leans up and smacks a quick kiss on the bodyguard's mouth.

Instant jealousy surges through me at their open affection for each other. I want that—desperately want it with Callum and Dom. But I know we can't—not until we three talk... if that ever happens.

A doctor approaches me, the man frowning deeply as his eyes zero in on my arm. "I'm Dr. Kim, the attending physician. Jana, is there a room free so I can get a better look at the wound?"

"Room three, Dr. Kim," the nurse says as she opens the door adjacent to where we are standing and then leaves.

John and I follow the doctor in and a moment later, the same nurse returns with a small tray. She sets it onto the movable table. "Have a seat, Mr..."

"Pen," I say and sit on the hospital bed.

It doesn't take Dr. Kim long to stitch me up. While he does, I fill John in on what happened. Three stitches later, the doctor's done, and we head back to Callum's room, where the Warrior Black security team is huddled in the hallway in front of the door. Neither detective is around.

"Did Longe and Faller get anything out of the shooter before the cops carted her out of here?" Dom asks Tobias.

"No." Tobias frowns. "She's claiming she's innocent. You shouldn't have touched that gun."

"Well, excuse me. Guess I wasn't thinking when I saw

her walk in, pull out a Beretta tapped with a silencer, and aim the fucking thing at us," Dom seethed. "Does Dante know?"

"Yep. And they are fueled to blow. Dante can't believe that this hospital's security is so shitty. They have a call scheduled with the record company and the hospital administration, but I'm sure we will hear from the band manager soon enough."

"Who was the target?" Fig asks, but the glint in his dark green eyes says he knows.

"Callum was the target," Dom says, rubbing the back of his neck. "Thank God for Pen reacting as quick as he did or..."

"Pen took the hit instead," Tobias says, looking at me. "All good?"

"Yeah."

"Stitches?" Dom looks at the bandage peeking out from under my bloody sleeve, his eyes filled with... Worry?

"Three." I say, but I'm taken aback by his show of emotion.

"Good."

"Keep it clean and dry, Mr. Gallagher," the doctor says as he moves through us on his way into Callum's room. I nod in acknowledgement.

A few minutes go by before Danny comes out and says, "Callum wants out."

We head inside the room, where Callum is arguing with Dr. Kim.

"I don't feel safe here. I want to leave," Callum insists.

"Fair to say, you're not going anywhere," the doctor blusters. "Now gentlemen, we only allow two people at a time. I need to have some of you leave the room—"

"I'm not leaving," Danny insists, folding his arms across his chest.

"Neither are we," Connor, Rafe and Bobby say in unison.

"We are their security, Dr. Kim. We aren't leaving, especially now," Tobias states firmly.

"I'm sorry, I—" Dr. Kim starts, but Dante strides in and cuts him off.

"*I'm sorry*, doctor, since your hospital didn't take proper precautions on my client's safety, I must insist you sign Mr. Fitz out of hospital, so we can take him to a proper facility that will secure his protection. If you don't, then I must insist you get the hospital administrator here—who I have already talked to, because I'm about to call the band's lawyer and then you will have a whole other set of issues on your hands." Dante didn't even bat an eye or take a breath as they put the doctor in his place.

Dr. Kim glares at Dante, then glances around the room at the security team, each one of whom is bulkier and at least six inches taller than he is. The doctor harrumphs and gives in. "Fine. Give me five minutes to put the paperwork in order, with instructions." He then storms out of the room.

"Geez, *fine* seems to be the word of the day," Danny chimes in.

Bobby pulls the ever-present sucker from his mouth and adds, "No kidding," before turning to Callum. "Seriously, dude, how are you feeling?"

"Aside from Dom smothering me while some crazed woman tried to kill us, I'm good." Callum glances at me. "How's your shoulder?"

"Don't worry. I'm stitched up and good," I admit with a smile, trying to ease the worry from Callum's frowny face. My feet automatically move until I reach the bedside and touch his cheek. "Do you need help into your clothes?"

Silence.

That's when I wince, drop my hand and slowly look

around me. Every pair of eyes are on us. Some faces show surprise, some wear huge smiles. Some are smiling huge. But one is frowning. Yeah, Dom is definitely not happy with me.

"Really?" Danny snickers, then his eyes darts to Connor and his right hand shoots out toward the drummer. "Pay up, asshole."

"Fuck me," Connor whines and shoves his hand into his pocket and pulls out a fifty dollar bill.

"What am I missing?" I ask, my attention landing on Dom, who's still scowling at me.

"You two..." Rafe's words hang in the air like a sharp sword.

I open my mouth to explain there's nothing between us, but no words come out.

Then Callum blurts, "No. We aren't together, Rafe. Stop making shit up."

And those words hurt more than the pain from the gunshot.

Chapter Eleven

Christ. I told Pen to be discreet about our plans for Callum, and here he goes looking like a lovesick pup around the rest of the security team and the band. Tobias is going to have his balls—and mine, if Pen doesn't pull his head out of his ass.

Granted, Tobias has no place to say shit. He fucking took Danny and ran two years ago, because of a stalker—Danny's former personal assistant, who was delusional and obsessed with the lead singer. By the end of the whole crazy fiasco, our lead ended up with Danny as his life partner. So no, he can't say shit to us.

Not wanting Pen to be singled out, I walk over to the opposite side of Callum's bed, silently admitting that yes, there is something going on with the three of us—even though Callum won't admit his feelings.

"Dom. Pen. Hallway, now." Tobias doesn't leave room for arguing as he strides out of the room. John follows behind him, his face a mask of indifference. But I see the corners of John's lips tip up—he too, has nothing to say about hooking up with a band member.

I turn to Pen and frown. "We're going to talk later about being discreet." I drop my scowl and glance at Callum with a reassuring smile. "Need anything?"

"Like that'll happen," he says flatly, his eyes never meeting mine. Callum's avoidance tactic won't work on me. I kiss the top of his head and walk out of the room, with Pen on my heels.

As we four stand outside the hospital room, we eyeball each other like we're in a stand-off. I can only imagine what the passersby are thinking as they look at us. Yes, we are an intimidating group.

I decide to put it out there. "Before you utter a word, Tobias, think about what happened two years ago with Danny," I say, holding nothing back.

"There's a difference," he growls low. "Danny and I weren't intimate when all that started."

"It doesn't matter." I glare, folding my arms across my chest. "Pen and I aren't giving Callum up, just because you tell us to. It's not your place to decide what we do."

"Maybe you two should—" John begins, but Pen whips his attention to the second lead and frowns.

"You have no room to talk either, Brand." Pen mimics my stance. "Do you have amnesia or something because I distinctly remember last year. The lengths you went to when Connor's uncle was threatening him are still very vivid in my mind."

"I know, I know," John utters in a reassuring tone. "What I was going to say," he looks pointedly at Pen, "is that before you get too deep into whatever you three have started—or not started, find out who is after him and why. Then you're free and clear to pursue whatever relationship you want without any chaos impacting your bubble."

"John's right. Safety needs to be first—that's our job. Warrior Black is our priority," Tobias says with less vinegar.

"I know Callum and the band's safety has to be our priority—I'm not an asshole," I proclaim. "We don't want grief from you or from the rest of our team, or from Dean and his guys."

"Hey, if you three are meant to be, so be it. I won't give you shit about it, but I can't be sure Danny won't read you the riot act. He's very protective of his friends—especially Callum. Just saying," Tobias says with a slight shake of his head.

"Callum's safety always comes before anything else—including my feelings," I admit.

"I echo that," Pen chimes in with a nod.

With the four of us in agreement, Tobias asks Fig and Jordan to join our circle before announcing, "We're going to have to call Dean for help once again."

"Once he hears what happened, Dean won't have a choice," John adds, shaking his head. "Besides, it's not like he has to come here."

Pen's brows furrow deep. I have the urge to smooth them out with my thumbs and then kiss his mouth to erase the concern etched in the corner of his green eyes. Instead, I ask, "What's wrong?"

He glances at me and some of the worry disappears from his face. Then he turns to Tobias and asks, "Are Dean's guys coming to protect the entire band, or just Callum and Dom—since the attack seems to have been directed at them?"

My mouth drops at Pen's remark. Why does he think I

need protection? If anything, it should be Callum and him. The shooter aimed the gun at Pen after she didn't have a clear shot at Callum. "I think all three of us are in jeopardy, Pen," I admit resolutely.

"This protection is for everyone," Tobias declares. "We can't chance doing otherwise."

"I'm staying," Jordan chimes in. "Dante already had a word with Dean last night because he texted me not five minutes ago to remain here with the band."

Out of all of the bodyguards, Jordan is the quiet and aloof one. The native Chicagoan doesn't get involved in everyday band drama. He just protects Bobby, the keyboardist, when the band goes on tour.

"I have to say, Jordan. This is the most I've heard you talk," John says, chuckling.

The man shrugs. "There isn't usually much to say. Everyone else talks enough without me adding to the conversation."

That's true. The band tends to fill the air with chatter, especially when there's good gossip in the rock and roll industry.

"So is Dean coming?" I ask him, shifting the topic back to what we need to focus on.

"No."

I figured that. Dean's been taking care of Ron during his cancer treatments. We had *all* been surprised by that relationship.

"But we can count on a few of Dean's heavy hitters," Tobias says. "We will also have access to Levi, his tech guru."

"Ron. Fuck." Pen frowns, then drops his attention to the floor. "I need to call Ron."

Ever since Ron's announcement last year about his cancer diagnosis, Pen has called him almost every day to see how the old band manager has been doing. However, with the chaos of our trip here and then Callum's attack, it seems he forgot to call Ron yesterday.

"Be right back," Pen says, pulling out his phone and walking off.

I have the sudden need to follow him and see if he's okay. An emotional Pen isn't always rational, particularly when Ron's name is mentioned in the conversation. Pen's super close with the old band manager. They have a similar past—the reactions of their families when they came out to them almost mirroring each other, just thirty years apart.

The old manager took Pen under his wing when Pen came out to his family and they pretty much shunned him. Except these past few months, his mother has been calling and texting him. I don't know what all that is about, Pen won't tell me, but lately he refuses to talk to her.

"Be right—"

"I'll check on him," John reassures me and then walks off toward Pen's direction.

I want to argue that Pen is my man, and it's up to me to tend to his needs. But the cautionary gaze from Tobias has me staying firm in my spot.

"Fig, you're quiet. Got any input?" Tobias asks.

"While we wait for Dean's men, call Levi so he can start working on Callum's father's itinerary from the past six months. That way we aren't here holding our balls, while waiting for something to happen," Fig says, cupping his dick.

"Good idea," Tobias says. "But we need to talk to the detectives about that woman."

"She's a hitman—I know it, but who hired her is what we need to know," I say, my gut churning with fire and the need to punch something... Multiple times.

What if Pen hadn't been fast enough? That thought

keeps swirling in my mind. I don't care if I get shot, but Callum has had enough brutality for one goddamned lifetime.

"We have seven months—until Rocktoberfest, to find out who's behind Callum's attack, track down any leads about this female shooter and who she's affiliated with," Tobias says, strain in his tone.

"Jesus," I say, rubbing the back of my neck. The huge event in Black Rock, Nevada is what jumpstarted Warrior Black's fame. It's the one event they would never miss a chance to play. And the chaos there makes protecting the band nearly impossible. We *have* to wrap this up before then.

"What if we don't?" Fig asks. "What if there are more attempts on Callum's life?"

"We don't have a choice. However, if Callum's father is the cause of this, then we don't have to look too far to find the answers and extinguish any threats."

"Now that's a plan." Fig raises his hand for a high five.

Both Tobias and I stare at Fig like he's certifiably strange. Jordan just rolls his eyes.

"What?" Fig says as he lowers his hand, shakes his head and backs into Callum's room.

"Now the question is," Tobias's eyes laser in on me, "between the two of us, who's going to tell the band and Dante that the band will be locked down until the threat is cleared?"

"I think, as lead, you have a better chance of calming the masses with that bad news."

"It's what I live for," Tobias rumbles out, tilting his head up in frustration. "Let's get out of the hospital first before I tell the band about the extra security coming at us."

We decide to secure Callum's house in Evergreen, then

we'll let the complaints begin. Only I don't care, because Callum will be completely safe with friends around him, and Pen and I at his back, protecting him.

Chapter Twelve

Callum

"Callum, wake up—you're safe." Pen's voice jars me out of my nightmare. He's holding my right hand while Dom's holding my left. Jesus, not even twenty-four hours back in my own place before the nightmares start back up. I questioned coming back here, to the scene of my attack, but Tobias said this was the best place to protect us all.

I glance at them, then down at the duvet. It's been ripped along the seam. "I thought I was fighting..."

"It's okay, baby. I'll get you another blanket," Dom whispers, cupping my face. "Want some water?" I nod, since my throat is as dry as the Outback. After several long sips, the achiness eases from my esophagus.

"Feeling some pain?" Pen asks with a small smile.

I slowly shake my head. "A little. But I don't want any

meds. They make me restless and I feel even more exhausted when I wake up." I pick at the tattered duvet. "I'm sorry I woke you both."

"You didn't. I was making my rounds in the house when I heard your shouting," Dom explains, taking a seat on the edge of the bed.

"And I was laying on the sofa," Pen admits sheepishly.

"Oh..." I'm not sure what to say to that. Guilt hasn't stopped riding me for the past two days. One or the other of these two men have been by my side, watching over me while I heal from the attack. Tonight, as I look at their bloodshot eyes, I'm ashamed that I haven't told them how much I appreciate them being with me.

"Would you feel better if we stayed with you until you fall asleep?"

Pen's question throws me for a second. *Stay with me.* Do I want these men with me? In my bed? My big, king-size bed? Where every time I lay in it, my loneliness settles in my chest?

But that's just it. I may be lonely, but I haven't been alone for quite some time. Especially, not since the attack. Every time I close my eyes, my mind takes me back to when I was beaten up. Every time I look out the window, I expect to see someone standing there watching me. Or they're going to climb through my bedroom window and attack me while I'm asleep.

I slowly shake my head. I don't want to keep having these worries and fears. But if I ask them to stay with me, there's a different risk—I'm too tired and still too physically sore to hide my emotions from these two men. These two men I've come to care about. Yet I can't openly admit my feelings, because then they'll start in on being in a relationship again. The truth is, that terrifies me.

It's not that I don't love them—I do, maybe more than I've ever loved anyone—but saying it out loud makes it real. The moment I admit how I feel, it stops being safe. I saw it in the way Brian treated my mum.

There are expectations, labels, with a future I'm not sure I can promise. Commitment has always felt like a trap to me, even when they are everything I want. So I keep quiet, hoping they won't see it in my eyes when I look at them.

"I get it," Pen says, releasing my hand and stepping away from the bed. "We'll let you—"

My eyes widen, seeing the hurt across Pen's face. I realize he has mistaken my head shaking for *No, I don't want you to be with me.*

"Pen, I..." I swallow hard. "I want you to... lay with me —both of you." I blow out a breath and continue. "I feel... Safe when you both are around me. And the doctor did tell me to rest." I try to make light of the situation, but it falls flat.

"Are you sure?" Pen asks as he hesitates to come closer.

"Yes," I say earnestly.

A second passes before Pen takes unsteady steps toward the bed and removes his shoes.

I glance at Dom, whose phone chimes with a text. He takes his cell phone out, frowns and shoves the device back in his pocket.

"Who's that?" Pen asks.

"No one," Dom says, brushing Pen off as he gets up. "I'll let Fig know I'm going to be with you." Dom then leaves the room.

Pen stares at the door, a frown deeper than Dom's plastered on his face. He removes his shirt but leaves his pants on.

"You can take them off. I know it's uncomfortable to wear jeans in bed." I try to be nonchalant, hoping to persuade Pen out of his irritation with Dom. If I'm honest with myself, I want nothing between his body and mine.

Pen turns back to me, his brow hikes high and a smile appears on his handsome face. "Uncomfortable, huh?"

"Yeah," I say, trying to smile too, but my lips hurt too much.

"Really?" he questions. Pen doesn't believe me, but he's not calling me out for it.

The sight of his smooth muscular chest is revving my heart up, but it's my dick that's becoming unruly, leaving no room in my underwear. As much as I want Pen to fuck me—have both Pen and Dom fill me up, I don't have the energy. But it doesn't mean I can't have their hands on me, and I grin at the thought.

Pen pauses with his pants half off and he looks at me. "No messing around, Callum. Sleep, and I mean it," Pen says, and I drop my smile.

"I know. I'm not healed yet."

Dom enters the room, then closes the door, a soft smile inching across his handsome face. "The house is secured. Dean's men arrived and are patrolling the outside of the property. Fig is awake and will safeguard the inside. Jordan and John are getting a few hours of sleep."

"That's good," I say, his words easing my worries.

"It is," he replies then enters the walk-in closet and comes out with another blanket. He removes the torn one, throws it off to the side and then spreads the new blanket over me.

With only his boxers on, Pen slips in to my left. "How do you want to lay?" he asks me, as his eyes move to Dom, a questioning look across his face.

My attention shifts to Dom, specifically his jean-clad crotch, as he slowly—torturously slowly, lowers his pants. I lick my lips, remembering what that cock has done to my ass.

I turn my focus back to Pen, recalling what he asked me just moments ago. "Because of my splint, I'm more comfortable if I lay on my right side. We can spoon," I say, shifting until I can find a comfortable spot.

Pen tucks himself behind me. He slips his free arm around my waist while the other is under my pillow. A sense of safety surrounds me, and I settle back even closer to Pen. The gentleness he exudes wraps around me like a warm blanket.

Dom eyes us for a long moment and smiles. "You have no idea how beautiful you two look together. I want to pull out my dick and stroke myself while watching you two. I wish..." he groans instead.

I freeze at his unspoken words. Even though that would definitely take my mind off of the nightmares, and Dom did in fact jerk me off in the hospital, which felt phenomenal. There's no way I can have both their cocks up my ass tonight, especially with a house full of people. I remember how loud my screams of pleasure were the last time, when they were both inside me.

I utter, "I don't—"

Dom raises a hand. "I'm not implying we should fuck, Callum. You're still hurt and we need to have the big talk first, okay? But..." His eyes shift to Pen, and I look over my shoulder at him. Pen's eyes widen before they narrow on Dom.

Big talk? I don't know what Dom is referring to, but whatever it is, we're not having that either.

"If you think we're going—" Pen starts to say as he sits up.

"Remember what we agreed to about arguing in bed?" Dom says, his eyes unblinking.

Pen licks his lower lip, and drops his eyes down to the sheet covering his lower half. "No arguing in bed."

"Yes. But what do we do instead, sweetheart?"

I can see Pen's jaw muscles working, like he doesn't want to answer Dom's question. But I want to know. I clumsily roll over, then reach up and cup Pen's face, hoping to ease the tension I see there. "What is it?"

"We fuck it out until we stop being angry and then we talk," Pen confesses. "But that's not happening." He looks right at Dom. "It's not happening."

"I'm not saying we should, only that we don't go to bed angry." Dom carefully climbs into bed on the other side of me and sits so that he and Pen are face to face. "I'm sorry if you're still upset with me."

Pen doesn't talk, but lies down. I roll back over and he spoons me, his right arm around my waist. Dom stretches his body next me, adjusts his pillow and reaches his left arm to circle both of us. With our legs tangled, Pen's heat against my back, and Dom's gentle breaths fanning my face, I fall asleep within minutes, feeling utterly safe.

Chapter Thirteen

P^{en}

I'm restless and unable to fall back asleep, and listening to Callum's and Dom's slow, steady breathing only makes me more restless. I slide out of bed then watch them for a minute to make sure I haven't woken them. *God, I love those two.* I grab my clothes from the floor and creep out of Callum's room.

After I dress in the living room, I shrug on my jacket and then the grab the radio and ear piece. I slide open one panel of Callum's fancy three-paneled slider and head outside for some cold, fresh mountain air.

It's two in the morning, and all seems quiet. I set off to walk the perimeter of the four thousand square foot house, trying to work off some of this restlessness.

As I turn the third corner, I realize I have not spotted a single one of Dean's men. Every hair follicle on my head tightens, and it's not from the cold air. A prickly feeling of being watched sets my teeth on edge. I call Dean's lead, Joel.

"Check in, Joel," I whisper into the radio.

Nothing.

"Someone check in," I add, holding my breath for a moment. And still nothing.

This isn't right. I run inside, finding Fig and Tobias in the hallway.

"What's going on?" Tobias asks.

"Dean's team isn't answering their radio."

"No one?" Fig adds.

"Nobody is."

"Wake, Jordan—"

"I'm up," Jordan growls, his gravelly voice letting us know we've woken him—which is confirmed by his attire. Or lack thereof. He's got bed head and is standing there in his boxers and nothing else.

"So am I," John says while yawning. At least he's fully dressed.

"I'm joining the party," Dom says from behind me. I glance over my shoulder. He's dressed in jeans and a white tank.

God, I love it when he looks so casual and dressed down.

Okay, dick. It's not the time.

"Each of you grab a headset," Tobias orders. "Pen and Dom, head around the back. Fig and Jordan hit the left side of the house. John and I will take the right."

"Let me grab some sweats," Jordan says before he quickly disappears down the hall.

"Let's go." Tobias then heads out the front door with his second following close behind.

Dom and I quietly head to the back of the house through the slider. With practiced ease, because we've done this more times lately than I can count, Dom automatically flanks to the left and I go right, edging the backyard's perimeter—then we zigzag the lawn like a synchronized dance until we meet at the back fencing. There's no need for a flashlight since we surveyed and marked the backyard when we brought Callum back.

I know every inch of this yard without having to see the three massive, empty planter boxes, the inground covered pool and a hot tub.

"Fuck," I hear Dom in my ears. "Pen, behind the Ponderosa pine."

I don't like his tone and rush over to his location. There, behind the tall pine lay one of Dean's men. "Is he—"

"He's alive, but out cold," Dom confesses as he's bent down, two fingers to the pulse point on the man's neck.

"I found two, and they look tranqed," Jordan replies over coms.

"I found Joel," Fig announces. "He's out cold."

"We need to reassess what the fuck is going on here," Tobias says, then adds, "I have to wake up Dean."

In that moment, I'm glad I'm not the lead. Telling Dean Harper that his best men have been drugged will not be pleasant.

The next several hours are nothing but crazy chaos. Dean's lead, Joel has been on the phone with Dean, getting his ass chewed out. And Dante is up to their ears with calls from the record label.

The one moment of relief we had was when Dante stumbled out of their room, barefoot and sleep rumpled. None of us had ever seen Dante looking less than their best and, for one full second, there was silence. You could have heard the proverbial pin drop.

Dean's men finally came to and were pronounced uninjured by Lyric. Dante loudly gloated that they were right to bring Lyric onboard to provide medical help to the band—and, by default, the band's security.

Callum, thankfully, has slept through this. Tobias wisely steered us all into the game room, which is the room farthest away from Callum's. We do not need Callum to know right now that the security we promised him has been breached.

Despite the clusterfuck around me, I keep track of Dom and the subtle way he looks at his phone every few minutes. He's been texting someone, and in between his texts, he's reading messages. When he caught me watching him, he quickly put his phone back in his pocket and walked out of my sight.

That's it. I'm tired of waiting for Dom to tell me what's going on. What could he be hiding that he can't share with me? I tell him everything. I can't remain silent any longer. I need to know.

I find him alone in the office, looking over the new security system Dean sent over. Given the risk of others entering, I ask Dom to go outside with me, so we can talk in private.

"All right." Dom nods and follows me to the deck on the side of the house. With a sideways nod of his head, he tells Dean's man to leave. "What's this about, babe?" Dom asks, folding his arms across his chest.

"What are you hiding from me?" I bluntly ask.

His eyes narrow and his body goes taut. "What do you mean? I'm hiding nothing from you."

"Then why wouldn't you tell me where you were going the other day? Why haven't you said anything since you got back? All you said was that you went to help an old friend you used to work with. What the hell kind of explanation was that? I don't even *know* where you used to work! And who do you keep texting? Is it that friend? We're supposed to be together—share things. Don't you trust me enough to talk to me?"

The muscles in Dom's jaw jump before he looks away. He drops his arms to his side and lets out a long exhale. *I hit the mark.*

With Dom's shitty excuse for his whereabouts, his words-only apology, and then further lack of communication, my doubt about the depth of his feelings for me runs riot through my head.

"I do trust you, Pen," he says, finally looking at me. "I don't know where your doubts are coming from, but I'm not hiding anything from you. I told you the truth. I went to see an old coworker that needed my help. That's all."

"I know that's what you said. But ever since we arrived here, you're always checking your phone, texting someone—"

"Are you watching me?" His low warning tone is enough to make my own hackles rise.

"Yeah, I am. Hell, Dom—I don't know anything about your past. Any time I ask about what you did before Harper Security, you brush me off. You won't talk to me about it. I'm supposed to be your partner, here at work and as your boyfriend. I should know something other than these last two years-worth of your life that we've spent together. Let me in," I plead, as my heart begins to race.

"Jesus—"

"Dom! Pen!" Our names pierce the air. We both rush around to the front of the house and see Lyric frantically waving his hands as he talks to Tobias.

"What's wrong?" Dom reaches them first.

"Callum's mom called him, crying for help."

I don't wait for the rest of the explanation to react, and I barrel inside the house, toward Callum's bedroom. The second I enter I hear crying. "Callum."

"Mum, please." He's sitting by the window and reaches for me with his splinted arm. His face is pinched and tears are running down his cheeks. "We're coming, Mum."

I take the phone from Callum and put it on speaker. "Mrs. Fitz, this is Pen Gallagher, one of your son's bodyguards. What happened?"

"Some guy broke into my house. He was looking for my husband," she says tearfully. "The guy put a gun to my head, Pen, and told me to tell Brian to stay out of his business," she chokes out, fear lacing her words.

Dom storms into the room, with Fig and Tobias behind him. "Mrs. Fitz, this is Dominic Rossetti. Is the guy still there?" he questions, taking the phone out of my hand.

I step back, aggravated at how he grabbed the phone from me and proceeds to take over the conversation. But I give Dom the space, and find myself standing next to Callum, who takes my hand. His grip is tighter than before, and that's a good sign. At least, for his healing.

I glance at his tear-stained face and my heart aches for him. I gently wrap my arm around Callum's shoulder while we listen to his panicking mother.

"No. He left, but I'm scared that he'll come back. And I don't know where Brian is—what if that guy wants to kill him? I don't know what to do."

"We can't worry about Brian right now. Our priority is you." Dom's voice has a hard edge, but then he gentles it enough to soothe her as he makes his plan clear. "Here's what I need you to do, Mrs. Fitz. Call the cops and let them know you had an intruder. Then go pack a bag. Someone from the Chicago Sentinel Agency will come pick you up.

They're friends of mine, so don't be alarmed when they show up. If you're not sure, call us, and we will verify them. They'll keep you safe until we can get to you. Do you understand?"

"Okay," she says, her sniffles echoing through the cell phone.

"Good. Here's Callum." Dom passes the cell to him and then he pulls out his own phone, taps the screen a few times and puts it to his ear. "Leo." He then strides out of the room just as the rest of the band runs in and stations themselves around Callum—and me because he still has a stranglehold on my hand.

I'm damn curious who Leo is, and the Chicago Sentinel Agency too. Is Leo the former coworker he keeps texting? Was that agency his former employer? An ache forms in my throat, but I gulp it back. Do I really know the man that I've been sleeping with? That I thought I was in a relationship with? If this thing with Callum hadn't come up, would Dom ever have told me about his past and the people he knows?

Jesus, why can't everything just go back to the way things were? Then I'm brought up short as I realize that I'm partially to blame—I'd been so happy to finally connect with someone, someone who accepted me as I am, with my insecurities, that I never even *asked* about his past before.

"I'm going to hang up, Mum. Call the cops like Dom said to do, then pack a bag. Call me when the security people pick you up, or before that if you get scared."

"Alright, my boy. I love you," she says and hangs up.

Callum clutches the phone to his chest. I try to release his hand, but his fingernails bite into my skin. "Please," he whispers, I'm not exactly sure what he wants, but anxiety coats his plea. He glances down at our joined hands and gasps. "I'm sorry.

"You didn't hurt me," I admit, and bend slightly toward him. "Your mother will be safe. Dom's on it. Okay?"

Callum calmly nods, but the desperation and tears in his eyes say otherwise. "Why is this happening to me, Pen?"

"I don't know. But we're doing our best to find out." I call the singer over to me and transfer Callum's hand from mine to Danny's before I stride from the room to find Dom.

Who is nowhere in sight. Instead, I'm met with an odd scene. Tobias is on the phone, talking very quietly, while the rest of the guys are scattered about the living room. Everyone is silent and they seem to be on edge. Fig glances at me, then points to the front door. I give him a single nod and head out to find my partner on the other side of the door, texting.

"Who's Leo?" I interrupt his texting.

This isn't jealousy—not completely, anyway. But all of a sudden, people from his past are coming out of the woodwork and I don't have a fucking clue who they are to Dom. Friends? An ex-lover? An old coworker?

I wait for a response, but Dom doesn't answer, nor does he stop texting—which spurs my anger. With every second, the tension in my chest tightens and I'm getting a headache from how hard I'm grinding my teeth together.

"Damn it, Dom. Answer me," I practically shout, not wanting to let this go until he tells me what I need to know.

He meets my eyes with a fiery glare, his nostrils flare and his body stiffens. "Can you give me a moment while I text the address to my friend, so he can pick up Callum's mother?"

His tone is like a slap across the face. Remorse and regret swirl around me as I step back, spin around and head inside the house. His abrupt words and his tone of voice clearly leave no doubt that I'm not worth the time or the explanation.

It's suddenly crystal clear that keeping me in the loop... of *anything*, is not a priority of his. And I'm also coming to realize that maybe Callum is right, and this throuple I wanted so badly is too good to be true.

I've poured my heart into the relationship I have with Dom, but I see now that the commitment has been lopsided. The realization that Dom doesn't value our relationship with the same weight I do hurts more than I can explain.

It hits me that this imbalance is what's been bothering me for a while, yet I'm still not ready to let go. Even if it feels like I'm the only one making an effort. The idea of walking away —of breaking up—tears at my soul, and in only the few seconds I've contemplated it, it's already created a deep, aching loss that I can feel in my bones. I begin to panic.

I need space. I have to leave. Breathe in fresh air and clear my head before I say or do something I'll regret.

"Pen, wait." I hear Dom call my name, but I ignore him. I head straight to Tobias.

"I'm sorry but I need a day," I say to my lead, who looks just as startled as his second standing next to him.

"Pen," John begins to say, but I shake my head and return my attention to Tobias.

"I only need today and will be back here first thing in the morning."

"What about Callum?" Tobias asks, then his eyes jump to someone behind me. Dom.

"You can't leave. Callum needs us," Dom insists as he grips my shoulder, trying to turn me around.

I yank out of his hold and do not look at nor respond to Dom. My focus remains on Tobias, silently pleading for time away from here. From Dominic Rossetti.

"Be back by eight a.m. tomorrow," Tobias conveys with a frown.

"Thanks." I turn, and John tosses me a set of keys.

"The Suburban in the driveway."

"What the fuck," Dom hisses. "Pen, where the hell are you going?"

I still don't answer him, which gives me a perverse sense of satisfaction for doing the same shit to him that he has been doing to me. Now that I think about it, Dom has used this evasive tactic several times in our relationship.

As much as it is not like me to be petulant, Dom gives me no choice but to leave. I need to get away from him so I can think things through. Our relationship, and maybe even this job.

My silence doesn't deter Dom, as he follows me. "For fucks sake, answer me, damnit."

I open the driver's side door, and climb in, but he blocks me from closing it.

"Move out of the way, Dom," I demand, trying to keep the bud of emotion that's stuck in the back of my throat from unfurling.

"Babe, talk to me—please." The tone of his voice is gentle and pleading. But where was his willingness to communicate before? Now that I'm leaving, he wants to open his mouth and talk? I don't think so.

"*Now* you want to talk to me? You know what? You're a selfish bastard. Taking and taking but never giving back. You walk away from me without a single word. Send and get text messages. Refuse to talk to me about any of it. No, you had your chance—a lot of chances, actually, and I'm done waiting," I spit out.

I'm too tightly wound to continue. I clamp my mouth shut before more hateful words come out. I start the SUV and buckle my seatbelt, avoiding his penetrating gaze.

Seconds pass before he finally steps back. "Alright. I'll give you the space you need."

I glare at him. *He is giving me space? Ha!*

I slam the driver's door, put the vehicle into drive and the pedal to the floor before he's even let go of the door. I barrel down the driveway without looking back. Because if I do, I won't leave. I'll be the same old Pen and give in to my desire to stay and talk to Dom. And he'll be the same old Dom with the same old half answers and nothing will have changed.

Chapter Fourteen

D om

As I watch my boyfriend drive off, I silently berate myself for being a giant dick. Would it have killed me to explain who Rick was before I left the hospital? Or put Leo on speaker so Pen could hear our plans for getting Callum's mother to a safe place before whoever's after Brian comes back?

Then again, it appears I have a habit of assuming that Pen will wait until later for his inquisition. Yet when the time comes for answers, I deflect. When he asked about Rick, I deflected. Tonight? I didn't even deflect about Leo, I was just plain rude and condescending.

Now I guess he is done with waiting. Pen has every right to ask those questions of a boyfriend. It's my insecurities that are keeping me from explaining myself. Or talking about my past with the military and my career with the U.S. Marshals. Hell, I even avoided his enquiry about my scar.

Shit. I'm a real prize, aren't I? I've also been assuming a lot lately, and as Pen pointed out, he's getting the blunt end of a raw deal. If running away from me is his only option, then I need to fix things between us before I lose him for good. But how?

I turn around and realize that we had an audience. I stride over to Tobias and get into his face. "Why did you let him leave?"

"Back, the fuck, up," Tobias seethes, straightening to his full height. He might be a few inches taller than me, but I'm far from intimidated.

"I asked you a fucking question." I don't move, but John gets between us, arms out and splitting the space.

"Come on. We need to have cool heads to think," John says in his calm demeanor, which I usually appreciate but is irritating the hell out of me right now. "We have someone coming after Callum. And the focus is on Brian. Let's put our energy toward that."

Fig approaches and says, "If you want, I can trail Pen."

"No. He'll be back tomorrow," Tobias relays quietly. "Get the guys to start packing things up. Most of us are heading out in an hour."

"Most?" Fig and I ask in unison, but I can't hide the irritation in my voice.

Tobias looks from me to Fig. "You two and Jordan will stay here with Callum. And once I get the okay with Dean, some of his men will also remain here. The rest of us will head to another secure location." Then Tobias turns to me. "Dom, we need to talk, alone."

"Fine," I bark.

"Do I need to be there to referee?" John asks, looking between Tobias and me.

I shake my head, and so does Tobias.

"We're good," Tobias relays and walks farther down the driveway until everyone disperses. I follow until Tobias turns and glares at me. "You're losing your shit, Rossetti. I need you to keep a cool head—just like John advised."

"I'm trying but when I see my teammate—"

"Let's be clear, Pen is more than your teammate. You know that, I know that... the whole goddamn team and the band know that. You're emotional. We all see it."

"What the fuck would you have me do?"

"Damn it, Dom, you're usually the one with the unruffled demeanor. But right now, you look half-cocked."

I rake my fingers through my short hair, scratching my scalp, frustrated and fucking annoyed. "Well, I can't help the way I feel."

"What I *need* to know is why did Pen feel he had to leave? It can't be because of Callum."

This isn't what I expected Tobias to say. I assumed he'd be pissed that Pen and I are together—and wanting Callum as our third. Our entire situation—our relationship as a couple and a possible and a possible throuple, is open for everyone to gawk at, and I don't like it. I'd prefer privacy but it's apparently a little too late.

I blow out a heavy breath. "I'm keeping shit too close to the vest," I finally admit.

"I get it. Can't say as I'm surprised. But there's nothing you can do about that until Pen comes back. Right now? This isn't the time to fucking lose your cool. Keep in mind what's going on around here." Tobias's eyes narrow on me as he makes a circular motion with his index finger, and suddenly my entire body is on alert.

"What is it?"

Tobias lowers his voice to an almost whisper. "John found some listening devices. He destroyed the ones he found, but he doesn't think he found them all. So from now on, be very careful when you speak inside the house. If it's at all related to any information on Callum's case, take it outside, and away from the house."

"You think whoever attacked Callum and is coming after Brian might have placed them?"

"I can't be too sure who placed them or when, but I'm leaning toward it. And John agrees."

"Jesus Christ. Alright. What else?"

"Dean called earlier. He conveyed that Levi found some dirt about Brian Fitz's past."

"What was Brian involved in?" I can only imagine the shit that bastard got into.

"Back in Australia, Brian was hanging with this group connected to drugs, gun running, and human trafficking. From what Levi dug up, Fitz got caught for selling illegal firearms to an Aussie undercover agent. Once the NSW police task force discovered who Brian was associated with, they leveraged him for information about the group."

"What's NSW?"

"New South Wales. Their task force is the equivalent to our DEA."

"So NSW gave that asshole options." I don't need a confirmation from Tobias to know what he's saying is true.

"Yes, they did. The task force wanted to bring this organization down with prejudice, and this was their in. Brian bargained for his freedom in exchange for ratting out the group. That's why he was able to flee Australia with his life, but he's never been allowed back on Aussie soil—Levi's words."

"Damn." I rub the back of my neck. I don't think Callum or his mother know of Brian's history or why he left Australia —well, not the extent of it anyway. "You think this group is after Brian and his family for payback? Even after all this time?"

"Dean thinks it's a good lead to follow," Tobias says, looking around us.

"Brian has to be the common denominator in all of this," I say. I turn to leave when I catch sight of Fig standing there, listening.

"Sorry," Fig says unapologetically. "Everything is almost packed, but Danny's arguing with John about leaving Callum here alone. I'm telling you, if your guy keeps it up, you're not going anywhere—not without Callum." He shakes his head.

"He's not going to be alone," I growl in Fig's direction.

He raises his hands up in surrender. "Don't bite the messenger."

"I'll talk to Danny," Tobias says and turns back to me. "We good?"

"Yeah." My shoulders drop as I breathe out, the tension easing. I just have to wait for Pen to get back and my groveling will begin.

"Where there's smoke, there's fire," Fig utters, staring off at Tobias, who's face to face with his irate boyfriend. Dante is also standing there, their face pinched in agitation.

Not sure what he meant by that, but sometimes what Fig says doesn't make sense.

"The label wants the band out of here, in case..." Dante finally says, but I get what they are saying.

"In case his attacker comes back to finish the job." The label has money riding on the band, and they don't want any of them to get hurt, or worse. And again, I get it.

For the next few minutes, the discourse between Tobias

and Danny is loud and clear. Then Tobias shuts his boyfriend up with a smoldering kiss that makes even my dick go hard. And... It works. Danny's malleable. But I have a feeling his compliance won't last long.

Tobias walks back over to me and pulls a set of keys out of his pocket and dangles them from his index finger.

"What's this?" I stare at two silver keys threaded onto a thick ring.

"The keys are to my lake house. I don't think this place is safe enough. Furthermore, you'll be closer to San Francisco—to us. So as soon as Pen gets back, go there until we can regroup and figure out who is behind all this."

"Are you sure?" I ask, gripping the keys tight in my hand like they are a lifeline.

"Yes. While Dean's men track down Brian's location, Callum needs to be in a safe place. This isn't it."

"I agree, but is your place secure enough?"

"Yeah, it is. Don't worry about anyone getting onto the property, there are sensors along the perimeter. If anybody decides to come onto the land, you will be notified of it. Each building also has sensors on the doors and windows. Trust me, after all that shit with Danny, it's the safest place on earth."

"Sounds like it's where we need to go," I say with relief. "Thank you." And for the first time, my gut isn't twisting up on how to protect my two men.

"There's a small cabin near the front end of the property, for Fig, Jordan and Joel and three of Dean's men—Patch, Pete and George. It sleeps six so they'll be fine. Lyric will stay with you, Pen and Callum in the lake house. There's plenty of room and space," Tobias says with a smirk. "And there's a he-shed—"

"Umm—what? A he-shed? You mean a she-shed?"

"No. I mean it's a he-shed—Danny—"

"Don't have to explain, I get it." I smirk. "Thanks—but Pen..."

"Give him this time. He'll be back tomorrow. Then tell him what the plan is. And Dom?"

"Yeah?"

"I know that peace of mind comes with control. But sometimes, not having all the answers and being *open* is what is needed for a relationship. I learned that the hard way," Tobias glances at me and gives one quick nod before walking away, leaving me contemplating my next step.

Although I see the truth in what Tobias just said, the knot of apprehension continues to grow in my chest. Right about now it feels about the size of a grapefruit. What if Pen comes back and tells me he's done with me? Or he'd rather be only with Callum?

I shake those dark thoughts out of my head.

Focus, Rossetti.

Callum's safety needs to come first. When Pen gets back tomorrow, I need to remind him of our goal, because if what Tobias said is true, then Callum is in bigger danger than I anticipated.

Until then, we need to be extra-vigilant, because with Pen gone, Callum's protection detail is one man down and we're more vulnerable. With Pen being pissed off at me, he won't answer my calls or text messages. Although I don't know how effective Pen would have been if he'd stayed, given his irrational frame of mind.

Then it hits me—Pen is in danger too, for going out on his own. He has done this before—retreat to clear his head. Just like Callum, he... Damn. Why haven't I realized this before? Maybe that's why I'm drawn to the bassist, too. Though they seem different as night and day, some aspects of their personalities are eerily similar. Each time Pen has left, he was upset and needed to think, and when Callum was upset after our night together, he fled to *his* retreat here.

And I know from past experience that when Pen is pissed off at me, he won't answer my calls or text messages...which is exactly what happened when Callum ran. *Jesus, I can't believe I didn't see this before.*

This is all my fault. Why can't I be open and share things about my past? Explain who Leo is. Tell Pen that I was in the Marines. Or tell him shit about my career as a U.S. Marshal before I was thrown out—hell, tell him about my sobriety. Who Rick is to me.

I got so caught up in what was growing between us that I ended up having tunnel vision. A year and a half into our relationship, and I'm just realizing I haven't made time for just us. Time to tell Pen that I love him. Yes, I love Pen. Fair to say, I've never said those words out loud.

Pen's correct that I'm a selfish bastard. I'll rectify that starting tomorrow, I assure myself as I head to the house.

The next hour is a flurry of activity as we secure bags in the vehicles Tobias has rented. He even switched out the Bronco I rented earlier for a Suburban.

Once the band and their security finally say their good-byes and leave, Fig goes back inside the house, while Jordan and Dean's men guard the perimeter of the property. I remain planted on the walkway, glancing down at the keys Tobias gave me.

"Dom." Fig calls from the doorway, which pulls me out of my thoughts. "Are you going to stand out there all day?"

Maybe.

I reluctantly meet Fig's golden eyes, expecting to see condemnation. Maybe even pity. Instead, I see none of the disappointment I'm expecting. Only detachment. Which strikes me as odd, but I'll take it over the other options any day.

"Callum's asking for you," Fig says. Did I hear annoyance?

"While you two talk, I'll make sure Callum has his stuff in order so we can move out by nine tomorrow," Fig says, then turns to go back in.

"What—who are you talking about?" I ask but Fig has already closed the door.

"I think he means me."

I spin around and find Pen standing on the driveway.

"I had to come back," he says evenly. "For Callum."

"I'm glad you're back," I say with some warmth.

Pen's chin tilts in defiance, and his arms remain folded across his broad chest. His rebelliousness has me smiling, even though that damn grapefruit is still in my chest.

Out of my periphery, I see a postal vehicle slowly coming up the driveway, but don't think much about it, assuming that Jordan or anyone of Dean's men would have cleared it. Until all hell breaks loose.

Just as Callum screams from the doorway for us to get down, a shower of bullets ricochets all around at us.

Chapter Fifteen

C allum

Against Lyric's wishes for me to stay in bed, I come out to the living room to talk to my friends before they leave. Especially Danny, who is upset about the plan. Now that they are finally out the door, I move to the window to watch the always-comical battle of who-gets-to-sit-where. Danny gets car sick if he rides in the back, so he's always riding shotgun, and Tobias doesn't let anyone but him drive the car Danny's in, so they sort themselves out pretty easily.

I'm distracted for a moment by a glint of metal through the trees, between the house and the road. Once I see that it's just the postman delivering mail across the street, I return my gaze to the driveway drama.

Bobby pulls the ever-present sucker from his mouth, bops Rafe on the forehead with it, and then scoots past our distracted guitarist to claim shotgun in another vehicle. I chuckle. God, I love those guys. And given the tenseness of the last few days, it's good to see my friends cutting loose a little.

I hope this separation doesn't stall Danny and Connor as they try to finish the three songs they claim to have started. We want to complete the album well before September, like planned. Then we can settle into the routine of the mini tour Dante has set up to promote the new album and showcase the playlist at Rocktoberfest. I can't wait.

After another entertaining ten minutes, I watch the caravan finally pull out of the drive, only to see that same glint in the distance. I look closer and it is the postman again. *Weird.* I would have thought they'd be done with this street by now, since my mail is delivered to my P.O. box in Denver.

I glance at Fig, who remains by the door and ask, "Can you get Dom to come back in? I want to talk to him."

"Sure," Fig says and pulls the door open and shouts at Dom. "Are you going to stand out there all day?" Apparently, Dom needs convincing. "Callum's asking for you."

Great. Now Dom thinks I'm needy. Thanks, Fig.

Out of my periphery, I see a Suburban pull up, and am confused for a minute assuming it's one of the vehicles that left with the band, until I see Pen. He gets out, a frown cemented in place, and starts walking toward Dom. Pen doesn't look happy.

"While you two talk, we'll make sure Callum has his stuff in order so we can move out by nine tomorrow," I hear Fig shout and then he comes back in.

Since I can't hear Pen and Dom, I resign myself to watching the back-and-forth between them through the window. I don't know what they are saying, but it looks heated.

"Now that the boys are gone, why don't you go rest," Lyric says once again.

"Please don't fuss over me, I'm feeling good," I assure my nurse, who's pouting.

"It's my job to fuss. Besides, I don't want Dante to fire me."

"Dante won't fire you," I say and return to watching Dom and Pen.

When I see the same postal vehicle turning into my driveway, every alarm in my head goes off. I move to the door and throw it open.

"What are you doing?" Lyric demands, following behind me.

"I don't get mail here," I frantically announce over my shoulder, stepping just outside the threshold.

As the postal vehicle speeds up the drive, I see the barrel of a rifle thrust out of the open window.

"Get down," I scream.

Suddenly I hear rapid gunfire as I'm being tackled from behind. My knees hit the ground first, and pain shoots up my legs. My chest lands in the grass, with my splinted arm is sandwiched between the two. My chin is the last thing to connect with the ground and I see stars.

When the sound of squealing tires fades, Fig growls in my ear, "Don't move."

"Callum," Lyric chokes out my name from my right.

I slowly turn my head and see Jordan on top of him, face to face with Lyric.

"Are you okay?" I reach my hand out to Lyric.

"I was going to ask you the same thing," he whimpers, then turns his attention to Jordan. "You can get off me now."

Jordan looks around, then he pushes away from Lyric, leaving the nurse looking as shaky as I feel.

Fig gets to his feet and carefully helps me up, but my vision whirls around and I'm about to pass out. Strong hands on my waist steady me. When my vision clears, I see it's Dom.

"Are you two alright?" Pen asks with trepidation. "Callum, you okay?"

"I'm good," Lyric replies, brushing off the back of his black pants.

I'm not okay. Far from it. But I lie. "Slightly banged my good elbow, but I'm okay." I rub at my right arm.

"Fig, get Callum back in the house," Dom commands. "Shit—Pen, you're shot."

"It's only a graze," Pen utters, glancing down at his thigh.

Pen's been shot twice now, thanks to that bastard. "I'm going to kill Brian, once I get my hands on that asshole," I grate out between clenched teeth. "This is all his fault."

"The vehicle is gone," one of Dean's men says as he pulls out his phone. "Want me to call the cops?"

Dom and Pen look at each for a second before Dom shakes his head. "No, Joel. We're not staying here. Get your team ready. Once Pen is patched up, we're out of here."

"You got it," he says and takes off toward the rest of his team.

"Where are we going?" I ask, as Lyric bends slightly to look at Pen's wound.

"It doesn't look bad, but I won't know for sure until he pulls down his jeans," he says, and that makes me laugh. Not a full belly one, but a soft chuckle that I can't help.

Lyric looks up at me, confusion on his face. "I'll explain when we get on the road."

I turn toward the house and freeze in place. "My house," I groan as I swallow down the rising bile. My home has bullet wounds. Everywhere I look, there are holes in the stone façade and cedar.

"Come on," Lyric says as he and Dom lead me to the sofa. I slowly sit, but my eyes are on Pen.

Dom looks around the room, like he might catch a ghost or something before his gaze settles back on me. "We're heading to San Fran," Dom says calmly. Although, I see there's an underlying hard edge to his jaw. He may not be happy about it, but I'm glad we're heading to San Francisco. At least I'll be with my friends. Then maybe I can call my mum and see how she's faring too.

"We think it's the safest place for you," Pen adds, looking around the room while Lyric cleans his wound. "But we're not saying anything more until we get in the car. John found several bugs in the house."

My eyes go wide—someone planted bugs in my house? No wonder Dom and Pen have been looking around the room.

"It's only a flesh wound," Lyric confirms as he slathers ointment over the injury, covers it with a big gauze pad, and then tapes it. "Done."

"Good. Now go pack up and be ready to leave in an hour," Dom says as he pulls out his cell phone.

"So, am I coming along for the ride?" Lyric asks with a pinched expression. The way his lips have thinned, I don't think he's ecstatic about the news.

"Yes, Lyric, you're coming with us," Dom says with a tone that brooks no argument.

"But I was told—"

Pen cuts Lyric off. "Like Dom said, you're coming with us. Please go get ready because we're leaving here as soon as we can."

"Is that going to be okay, Lyric?" I ask, feeling terrible that he has no say in the matter.

"Do I have a choice?" He stands, glaring at the two men.

"No," Dom and Pen say in unison.

Lyric huffs before he strides to his room and slams the door.

"He hasn't been here a full day, do you really think he needs to come?" I ask, eyeballing Dom, then Pen. "He has no idea what is going on. I don't want to bring another person into this shit."

"Too late. He's involved," Pen says sadly.

"All this is twisting my guts around," I say. I feel sorry for Lyric. He didn't ask for this. "I'm going to go pack," I announce as I get up from the sofa.

"Take only what you need," Dom replies, more earnest than before.

I shrug. "I didn't bring much, anyway." On my way to the bedroom, I turn and ask, "Will I be able to talk to my mum?"

"No. We can't take the chance just yet," Dom throws in, then comes close to whisper the plan for my mother.

After finding out that my mum has been taken to a safe house, I let out a breath and lean against the wall. "Why is this happening to me? And to her?" I cover my face with both hands and slowly shake my head. "I'm exhausted."

"Cal—"

"No, Dom. I've been holding my tongue for way too long. I'm tired. I was literally beaten up, then shot at and tackled, and now I'm being moved about like I'm some damn chess piece." I close my eyes to stem the tears that are threatening.

"Baby." I feel Dom move to my left and take my hand. Then a solid presence presses gently on my right side—Pen. Dom continues, "I promise—like I promised Pen, all will be explained once we get to San Fran. Please, bear it a little longer."

I open my eyes and study the men who snared my attention all those months ago. From the day each one of them started working for Warrior Black, they have been there for me. They kept me safe through everything that happened with Danny's stalker and Connor's psycho uncle. And now they are trying to keep me safe from Brian.

Pen cups my cheeks and turns my face his way. "If I can wait for Dom's explanation, you can too." He then leans in and gives me a chaste kiss. His lips are warm and gentle, and full of promise. Full of hope that all this will be behind us soon.

"Okay," I whisper, and kiss him back. And then turn to Dom. "What do you need me to do?"

"Just gather your things. We will handle everything else, including locking up."

"And I'll talk to Lyric," Pen says, which eases my mind. Pen can have a gentle touch when talking to others, whereas Dom almost always comes at you like a blunt object.

Within a matter of an hour, we leave my mountain home and head to San Fran. Or so I thought.

Chapter Sixteen

Pen

After Dean's men thoroughly check all the vehicles for trackers, we get on the road. Dom, Callum, Lyric and I are in the Suburban Tobias rented for us. Jordan, Fig and Joel hop into the vehicle I took earlier, and the rest of Dean's men are in the Explorer they had brought.

Not fifteen minutes from the house Dom begins to explain to Callum and Lyric that we aren't heading to San Francisco. Instead, we'll be driving to Tobias's lake house in Bear Lake, California.

"I don't understand why you didn't say that back at the house?" Lyric asks, confusion across his face.

"We didn't want to tell you the truth in case there were more bugs in that place than what security had found," I explain.

"Lyric," Callum says sullenly, his eyes dropping to his lap, "we're not going to San Francisco because they are separating me from the rest of the band, so that whoever is after me, doesn't hurt my friends."

Lyric gasps. "Is that true?" he questions, his eyes sliding to the back of Dom's head and then back to me. "Is it?"

"Yes," Dom says as he gets on I-70, heading west.

Lyric leans forward between the front seats. "Then why didn't I get a choice about coming? I shouldn't be forced to be involved in this, especially if my life is in danger. I want out!" He turns and looks at me. "Callum, I'm sorry, but I can't go with you." Lyric's frantic pleading pulls at my heart. I don't blame him for wanting to get away from us. I wouldn't go either.

"You're right," Callum says somberly. He faces Dom and me. "I don't want him involved. Is there a way we can drop him off somewhere safe?"

"Are you sure?" I ask Lyric, hoping the nurse will change his mind on Callum's behalf.

"I'm positive." He straightens in the back seat, pulling his shoulder purse over his head. "There," he points to a Starbucks logo on a highway sign. "Drop me off there and I can get a ride back."

"Get on the radio and let the rest know we're stopping to drop off Lyric," Dom says to me.

I notify the rest of the caravan of what we're doing, and we agree that everyone else will continue on. It's a long drive —we'll catch up to them eventually.

Dom exits the highway near the town of Northern Evergreen and pulls into the Starbucks lot.

"Please call me, Callum, when you arrive safe," Lyric says as he gets out and then closes the door.

"Why in the hell does he want a call when he wants no

part of what's happening?" Dom scoffs, then adds, "Anyone want coffee while we're here?"

We go through the drive-through and then get back onto the highway. I call Dante, letting them know of Lyric's decision to not go with us. The air in the SUV becomes heavy as the band manager swears up and down, then hangs up.

"I never heard Dante swear before." There's a note of humor in Callum's voice.

"I'm sure this won't be the last time," Dom says.

Callum yawns and I notice his eyes are glazed over.

"Why don't you lean back and get some sleep," I suggest over my shoulder.

I can see he wants to protest, but Dom jumps in, agreeing with me.

"Fine," Callum says, as he hits the button on the side of his captain's chair, reclines the seat back, and gets comfortable.

Dom and I don't bring up the argument we had on the driveway, which I'm glad for, since I don't want Callum involved.

It's the next morning before our little caravan finally arrives at the entrance to Tobias's place in Bear Lake. Dom stops and enters the code for the gate—after everything Danny went through with his stalker, Tobias fortified the grounds, including perimeter fencing and coded entry gate. Once through, we drive a quarter mile until we pull up to the cabin where the security team will be staying. The trip took nearly twenty hours. Aside from a few pitstops for bathroom breaks, and to get gas and food, we drove through the night, straight to the property.

Everyone stretches and groans as we get out of the cars and Dom gives assignments to Fig, Jordan, Joel and to the rest of Dean's men. Once that's settled, Dom drives Callum and me a little bit farther down the road until we pull up next to a quaint house with a lake behind it.

As Dom and I haul our bags from the trunk of the SUV, Callum ambles his way around to the back of the house.

Dom gives me a simple head tilt to tail Callum. I follow him until we are standing on the deck, looking out toward the water. With a cool breeze sweeping in, he shivers. I take off my thin jacket and wrap it around Callum.

"Better?" I ask, hoping for a little smile out of the man. He's been quiet nearly the entire ride here.

"Thanks, yes." He glances at me and I get my wish. Then he turns back to gaze at the lake and takes a deep inhale. "I truly love this place. It's peaceful and I think I can definitely write some great songs while I'm here."

"I'm sure you can. Dom and I won't bother you, promise." I lean in and kiss his temple and then step back, so he can have more breathing room.

With his back to me, I admire Callum's tight muscular body. He's bent slightly, leaning on the railing as he looks out at the water, and it accentuates his rounded butt.

Memories from our night together crash down on me and I ache to show him how much I care. Yes, the sex was some of the best I've had—his sweet, tight hole sliding up and down my cock, his salacious moans as he choked on Dom's dick. But that's nothing compared to how this man's dry humor and earnest demeanor make me smile. There's so much more to us than sex.

"Pen," Dom calls to me, and I quickly clear my mind.

"Need anything?" I ask Callum, but he shakes his head without looking my way. I walk back around to the front of the house, and see Dom scanning the ground like he's dropped something. "What are you looking for?"

"A fake rock. Tobias didn't give me the key to this house,"

he says, his eyes trained to the brown mulch around the yew bushes.

"What does it look like?" I ask, joining his search.

"Brown and black. That's all Danny said." He looks at me and rolls his eyes.

"Is that it?" I point to a medium-size rock that is brown and black with white speckles.

Dom lifts the rock up and, sure enough, it's fake. He turns it over and there's a black rectangular box inside. With a gentle push of the lid, it slides open, exposing a silver key.

"Grab the bags," Dom says. I get what I can as he opens the front door. He comes back and grabs the rest of the luggage.

After we look at the two rooms, I agree with Dom that we should give Callum the master bedroom, with a separate bathroom attached to it. The master will give him privacy to compose his music without anyone intruding.

Reluctantly, I also agree that Dom and I will share the smaller room and its queen-size bed. I hesitate not because of the bed size, but because of what is still festering between us.

I go out to the deck to let Callum know his bags are in his room, and he follows me back in and starts unpacking. I head into the room I'll be sharing with Dom to do the same. Dom's just finishing, but instead of leaving the room, he sits on the bed.

"What's wrong?" Dom says quietly, probably so Callum doesn't hear us.

"Why are you asking?" So what if I sound petulant.

"From the time we got on the road, you've been cold and not really talking to me." Is Dom hurt by my lack of communication? Oh well.

"I'm not in a talkative mood." Fuck it. I can't unpack with Dom in the room, watching me. I need to think—maybe do a thorough walk about the lake while my emotions settle. I'm turning toward the bedroom door, when Dom clasps my forearm and turns me toward him.

"Where are you going? We need to talk." The demand in his tone is sparking my irritation.

I pull out of his hold and step back. "I'm going for a walk. Want to check out the lake," I admit and turn around to leave, but Dom gets in my path.

"I want to talk—we need to hash this out now."

"It's always on your terms, isn't it Dom? Well, not this time."

"What the hell is wrong with you. You wanted me to talk before and here I am, and now you want to walk away with a stick up your ass. I wish you would stop playing games."

His words land like a hard punch to my solar plexus—sudden, sharp, and breath-stealing.

"You think I'm playing games?"

Dom's chin drops to his chest and he gives a noisy exhale, before he lifts his head and meets my eyes. "No."

"Then what *do* you mean? It's not like *I* took off without letting you know where I was headed, not saying a word to you for twenty-four hours. And what's with these people coming out of the woodwork—old friends and coworkers I have no clue about because you don't talk about your past. What about the secret calls and text messages?"

"That's not fair," he hisses. "You took off without—"

"You were standing right there when I asked Tobias for some time. So don't go shoving that in my face." My voice rises into a near shout.

"What the hell is going on here? Why are you two fighting?" Callum asks, striding into the room, and standing between us. I didn't realize that I'd moved to stand chest to chest with Dom.

"It's only a disagreement. Don't worry about it, Callum," Dom says before stalking out of the house.

"What am I missing?" he asks, looking to me for an answer.

What do I say to this man I want in my life? This man who I had wanted to be with Dom and me—back when I thought there would continue to be a Dom and me? Do I tell him that Dom's keeping secrets? That he won't let anyone—especially me, in?

"Like he said, it's only a disagreement," I say, and leave before Callum questions me again. I leave the house, heading toward the lake for a walk that I hope to God will clear my head before my frustration and anger have me doing something I will truly regret.

Chapter Seventeen

C allum

I'm tired of laying in bed, but I feign sleep when I hear Dom open my bedroom door to check on me. Then I hear him quietly close the door, and my ears track his heavy treads until another door opens and closes. *One down, one to go.*

When I hear Pen's lighter steps approach, I close my eyes and again pretend to be asleep. Pen, satisfied I'm still resting, leaves my room and exits the house through the back slider.

Finally. I exhale and sit up, the movement easier than when we arrived three days ago. As much as I love them and their company, since we arrived at Tobias's place, they haven't been their usual selves.

They hardly speak to each other. It's almost as if they're intentionally avoiding any interaction unless it's absolutely necessary. It's incredibly frustrating and feels petty. I've tried talking to each of them, but neither is willing to discuss it with me.

Pen is as gentle as ever toward me, but every time I catch him watching Dom, I can almost *feel* a quiet anger simmering within him. I've asked him what is wrong, but he brushes off the question and walks away.

And this nonsense about the bedrooms? They decided I should have the master bedroom with its king-size bed while they're sharing the smaller room with a queen-size mattress. How ridiculous is it to see two big, hulking men—especially big, hulking men who are not getting along, sharing a small space. I keep thinking one of them is going to fall off the bed. I offered several times to take the smaller room, but Dom refuses and Pen just shakes his head.

Despite whatever beef they have with each other, though, they are both constantly checking up on me. It's comforting, and it's making me crazy.

I carefully get out of bed, and grab a pair of pajama pants and an old Night Rider t-shirt I've had forever. I pass a mirror that's hanging on the wall. After Connor made a comment in the hospital about what my face looked like, I made sure to avoid all mirrors—even the ones in the bathroom. Until now.

I glance into it and pause. This is the first time in a week I've seen my face, and it's still a little frightening. The image reflected back is a spectrum of colors, ranging from purplish blue to orangey yellow. It's an improvement on what Connor described, but it's still obvious I was beaten up.

The headache from the concussion is gone, my pain has eased some, too, and I can open both eyes now. What's still a mess is my ego—that got bruised up like a bitch. It's been years since someone has put the hurt on me like that fucker did, but at least I'm here and alive, which is the most important thing.

Before leaving the room, I put my ear to the door and listen. From the lack of noise, I assume I'm alone in the house. Though the panic in my gut is a constant reminder to be on alert, for the first time since we left my place in Colorado the need to relax is stronger.

I make my way into the kitchen and eye the dirty dishes piled in the sink. Dom and Pen's relentless insistence that I rest and not lift a finger to do anything around the place has become nerve racking. Sure, I'm still a little sore, but I'm as capable as anyone else. Especially Pen—the guy was shot twice but no one expects *him* to slack off. Hell, they won't even allow me outside to enjoy the late spring weather. It's righteously pissing me off.

At least neither of them has pushed for a discussion about a relationship—especially Dom. Maybe I'm giving off stand-offish vibes. Or maybe they've changed their minds about wanting me. While both are possible, I'd bet Dom's giving me time to wage war in my head before he approaches me on it. Damn. Guess that means he *does* know me pretty well.

If I'm honest with myself, the real reason for most of my irritability is simpler than I let myself believe. I'm starting to feel the ache of loneliness at night, an ache caused by being without them. I know they mean well, truly. But can't they see? I want them here, beside me. Yet I can't ask them to join me because that will give them hope and open myself up to *the relationship discussion.*

I give up on the idea of doing dishes and walk through the living area, taking in the changes to the space. It's been a while since I've been here, but this place is really trans-formed. Tobias and Danny have made the rustic house more like a home away from home. The original warm browns and golds are now accented with pops of vibrant colors that I'm sure Danny contributed to the place.

I feel myself slowly easing into the calm.

As I stand in front of the slider, looking out toward the dark of night, I take a slow breath in, and think. I've done enough resting. Right now, I need to focus on what's coming up for Warrior Black.

There's an album that needs finishing. Dante informed us last month that Ron has set up a few spotlight performances and appearances in the next several months. God, I miss that man. I hope he kicks cancer's ass and takes back his rightful place with us.

Don't get me wrong, I love Dante. They are formidable and know their stuff. But Ron is the one who made Warrior Black what it is today. A successful rock band. I don't want to let him down. This sitting around, doing nothing but resting, isn't in my nature. Especially when there is so much work to do. We are going back into the studio in two months to record the new album—and we are five songs—maybe six, short from completing the album.

And I can't forget Rocktoberfest in October, at Black Rock. When Dante told us Warrior Black had been invited back—again, it felt like we'd *arrived*. And this year's band line up is even more awesome than last year's. It's going to be fucking spectacular.

My excitement is crushed in the next breath, when I realize that if Tobias and Dean can't find out who is behind the attack on me, who hired the female hitman at the hospital, and who shot up my house, the label won't allow us to be exposed at Rocktoberfest or go on tour.

"Take a breath," I tell myself and slowly walk over to the Barclay loveseat.

I smile when I see that Dom or Pen has taken my song book from my bag and set it on the bladder-shaped side table.

And right next to it is my granddad's guitar resting on the stand.

The moment I catch sight of the instrument, my energy revs up and my mind automatically shift into music. I pick it up and then sit and lay the guitar across my lap. After a quick tune, I run a finger across the strings, pulling a familiar melody from the precious instrument.

Starting off with something simple, I replay the song I sang in the hospital. I softly croon the words my granddad taught me before I switch it to one of our latest songs—the one that hit number three on the Billboard chart.

As I close my eyes, new phrases of melody filter through my brain and I can see a song building in my head, along with the accompanying tune.

I picture what Rafe would play—jotting the notes down in the notebook. Then Bobby on the keyboard, and Wildman —Connor on the drums, until it comes together for me.

The interwoven sounds—practically a symphony of instruments playing like a concert in my head, but with no words. Yet.

Then I envision Danny on stage—mic in hand, and one by one, line by line, the words rush forth like water shooting through a break in a dam.

Note after note, word after word, this new song hits a certain part of my soul and I'm tearing up.

Though Danny was the person I pictured singing the song, the words are mine for Dom and Pen. No matter how much I try to ignore the fact that I've been falling in love with two men—for a while now, the idea of admitting the truth about my feelings makes me clam up. Every. Damn. Time.

But the song—this song can help me say what my heart wants to scream.

There's fire in their eyes as we dance in the dark.

The storm, the crash, the rush of my heart.
Three kinds of love built on passion's fire.
Three kinds of temptation—lust, craving, desire.
But love like that don't last too long.
I'm in for a heart break, or am I wrong?
One is a lesson, a fear to love.
One is of peace, a breath from above.
But I've no need of a spotlight, just need to be me.
The kind of love that sets my spirit free.
Three kinds of love built on passion's fire.
Three kinds of temptation—lust, craving, desire.
Unsteady ground I walk upon, learning life is a hardball
Misery is my company, moving blindly through it all.
One is a storm, one's a steady sea.
They shake my world, and set me free.
Three kinds of love built on passion's fire.
Three kinds of temptation—hope, respect, inspire.

I slowly lean back against the loveseat, the guitar laying gently on my lap and my head filled with emotion as my eyes rove over the exposed ceiling beams. Brian's nasty barbs about me playing bass and about my friends haven't stopped me from making music. Even through the pain, nothing stops the flow. With that thought, a smile crests my face as I close the notebook. I can't wait until my mates see this one.

As the words I've just written pour over me like liquid truth, I realize that I can't let fear dictate my life, especially where my heart is concerned. It's up to me to make the final decision on if I want these two men in my life. Want to form a relationship with them. Forge a bond similar to what I've seen Danny and Connor form with their men.

Truth is, no matter how much I have distance myself from them, Dom and Pen have never stopped treating me with respect. With that revelation, for the first time, I can breathe. There's a lightness in my chest and the heavy weight is gone.

They are nothing like Brian. And that thought shocks the hell out of me. Had that worry been percolating in my subconscious this whole time?

A noise from the door drop-kicks me out of my happy stupor. Pen walks in, a grim look across his face. I straighten; alarm shoots through me. "What's wrong?"

His head darts up, and it's obvious that he's surprised to see me. "Nothing's wrong." He frowns. "It's late. Why are you up?"

"I couldn't sleep," I admit sheepishly. "So I came out here to play and hopefully get inspiration."

"Did you?"

"Did I what?" I meet his eyes, which still have a hint of ire in their green depths.

He shakes his head and smiles. "Did you get inspired?"

"Yes," I say with a chuckle, then quickly sober. "Now tell me the truth. Why do you look upset?"

"It's nothing. Dom just—he's just frustrating sometimes... But don't worry about it."

I slowly get up from the loveseat and place the guitar in its stand. Pen reaches me in three long strides and I gently grip his hand. "Do you want to talk about it?"

I'm only an inch shorter than Pen, so we're almost eye to eye. As he stares into my eyes, a softness creeps across his face. "I promise you, Callum, I'm good." He leans in and kisses my nose.

That little gesture is what I love about Pen Gallagher. Looking at the muscular bodyguard, one would never guess that he's such a cinnamon roll—always thinking of others. But now he's gifted me that sweet kiss, and when a whiff of his brown sugar body wash is added to my sensory load, I'm suddenly craving his lips, and an actual cinnamon roll.

I smile huge at the image in my head. Pen laying naked on the bed with the bakery confection smeared across his body. And me, licking it up.

"What are you thinking about? Your face turned five shades of red," Pen says with a smirk. "And that's added to your blues, yellows, and greens."

No! Jesus. "Nothing." I feel my cheeks heat up even more.

"Now who's lying?"

I clear my throat and step away from Pen. "Where's Dom?" I look to the doorway.

"He went to talk to Fig and Jordan. He'll be back in an hour. Why?" His soft growl has me shivering.

Is he thinking what I'm thinking?

I don't know what to do. Should I say something? Or just come out and bluntly say what I want?

As I look at Pen, doubt begins to filter in, making me distrust my own feelings. I'm so attracted to him, but I'm equally attracted to Dom too. And I know they are each attracted to me, to the point that both want a throuple relationship. A commitment.

Could they be misreading their desires for me? Mistaking physical attraction for love?

I never thought I'd be in love with two men. But to give both of them my heart would expose me to hurt. Maybe I'm not ready to bare my feelings yet. Not until I'm sure they feel the same as me.

But that kiss. Pen's kisses are so sweet. Loving even. Not five minutes ago, I'd realized that it's up to me to make the final decision if I want these two men in my life, if I want to be in a relationship with them. And I do. Just how to convey that...

Pen's kisses. Can it be that simple?

"What are you thinking about?" Pen grips my hips, gently turning me—and a smile brightens his face.

"Kiss me." I reach out, sliding my hand around the back of Pen's neck and slowly bringing his lips toward mine, leaving mere millimeters between us, letting him decide whether we go any further.

"Oh yeah?" he whispers against my mouth, and a spike of lust shoots straight to my cock, leaving no room for disparaging thoughts. From the impressive hard-on he is pressing against the equally steely length in my pajama pants, he wants me as much as I want him.

This close, I can see a shift in Pen's eyes to something more electrifying. Demanding. A silent command for me to say yes. Giving him permission, like I did all those months ago when we first touched each other—it's a thrill for me. I might not be ready for a relationship, but loving on each other is what I've been hungering for. To take and be taken—it's what I need right now. To forget the world outside.

However, Pen pulls back slightly and studies my face. "You know I would love to worship you—make you feel good. But I don't think you're healed enough."

"I'm not asking you to, Pen. I'm telling you to. I need this —I need *you.*" I spell it out so he can't misunderstand me. Then I kiss him, hoping he gives in to my wish.

"Callum," Pen growls low. He leans in and kisses me back gently, dipping his talented tongue into my mouth before moving away. "I know that look."

I let out a sigh. "What look?"

"That look on your face. You have something up your sleeve," he says with a smirk. "What about Dom?"

"Dom isn't here," I whisper and take his mouth in a full-blown kiss, all lips, tongue and teeth. I don't care if my mouth and jaw still hurt a little. Something about the way Pen is cupping my cheeks so carefully has my heart bursting with more emotions.

Pen pulls back again and looks deep into my eyes. "Are you sure?"

"Hell yeah, I'm sure."

The second my words come out of my mouth, Pen wraps his arms around me and hoists me off my feet. With his mouth on mine, he carries me into the master bedroom.

With simple ease, Pen lowers me to my feet, steps back and commands, "Take off your clothes and lay down."

A shiver ripples through my body as I comply. Then I scoop up one of the pillows and tuck it behind my head as I lay on my back. All the while I watch my gorgeous body-guard take off his clothes.

First, he peels his skin-tight, black t-shirt from his broad chest and thick, ropey biceps. Then he lowers those jeans... *Holy fuck.*

My mouth drops open at the image before me. Pen is wearing a colorful sport jockstrap that has me drooling. He turns around, exposing his bare ass to me. "What do you think?"

"Damn," I utter, while liquid heat pools in my groin. I don't think I've ever been this hard while just looking at someone.

The one night Dom, Pen and I fucked, I was so out of my head—wanting to forget the terrible argument I'd had with Brian, I had stolen a bottle of Rafe's expensive Macallan and drank four shots. I'm such a light weight that I don't remember what their bodies looked like.

I didn't get to trace to memory of every dip and curve of my men's muscular frames.

My men—and I can say it clearly now because they *are* mine.

"Pen," I say with fervent need. I reach out my hand, needing the contact.

He laces his fingers with mine and climbs on top of me, straddling my waist. "Is this okay—am I hurting you?"

I shake my head. "No. I like it when you're on top of me."

He leans over, our cocks—separated by only his jock—rub together as he links his other hand into mine. "Now I have you, Callum Fitz. What should I do with you?"

"Love me." The words slip out of my mouth so easily that it doesn't dawn on me until Pen's eyes widen in surprise just what I said. "I-I mean—I would love—"

Pen slams his mouth onto mine as his body molds to me as though we're one.

His weight, the heat of his body and our intense kiss... and I'm done waiting. "Pen." Uttering his name is enough of a push.

Pen slowly makes his way down my body, licking, kissing and nipping along my tender flesh until he's at my erect dick.

"Hmm. I've been dying to taste you again." Without a moment's hesitation, he takes me into his mouth and sucks my tip.

I groan from the pleasure of that simple action. "Don't fucking stop."

"I won't baby." And then he sucks the tip back in before licking up and down my length. He grips the base of my cock and swallows me down the back of his throat.

I nearly let out a shout of desire, but I clamp my teeth tight and ride the wave of pleasure until I'm about to come.

Then Pen does the unthinkable. He pops off of me and says, "Don't come yet."

"What the fuck," I groan out in dismay.

"I promise you'll love this," he explains before he spits onto his fingers and presses one tip against my asshole. "Mmm. So tight."

A soft hiss leaves my lips as that single digit breaches my hole. Then he adds a second, and a pleasured pain courses through my lower half, but I need more. I shift my legs slightly wider apart and start moving my hips, getting the friction my body is craving.

"So fucking eager," Pen says as he presses a third finger inside me. "How does this feel?"

"Yes." I stretch my neck back, as his three fingers slide inside my body and have me riding the edge. "Fuck—yes—don't stop."

Pen chuckles, then drops his head and sucks my cock with hard, greedy pulls. I lose it right then and come like a geyser down his throat.

Not once does he pull his fingers from my body. "You taste like sunshine."

I bust out laughing, covering my eyes with my arm. "Pen." Not sure what else to say to his goofy praise.

"What? You do," he defends as he finally pulls his fingers out of my ass and lays down next to me.

"Okay," I say, and slowly turn to face him.

His smile is radiant and for the first time in a while, he looks happy. Then I realize that he's that way because of me.

"What are you thinking about?" he asks, touching my still bruised cheek.

I lean into his touch, but keep my eyes locked with his. "I wish I could bottle this moment up so I can pull it out later when I have a shitty day."

"Yeah?"

"Yeah."

"What are you afraid of with us, Callum?" That question startles me. Pen or Dom had never asked me why I fear this connection with them. Or why I'm so hesitant to form a relationship. But maybe this is the time to fess up to my trepidation. If I can't tell Pen—who is the most genuine and honest person I know, then who can I explain my fears to?

"Brian," I say softly, because I don't want his name to taint the moment.

"Your father?" Pen's eyes narrow slightly, and a glint of anger sparks in them. "What does he have to do with us?"

"You know how my parents are. They are constantly fighting. It was even worse back when we lived in Australia. My mum—as much as I love that woman, she could never stand up to Brian. He's a manipulating cunt, especially when he wants something. If it weren't for my granddad, we would probably be dead because of the bad shit Brian was into."

Pen opens his mouth, then shuts it like he wanted to say something but decided against it.

"What?"

"You knew that your father was into some heavy crap back then?"

I have to think for a second before saying, "All I know is what my granddad said to my mum before he gave us money to leave the country."

"And what was that?"

"The friends—Granddad used his fingers as quotes— Brian was hanging out with were a bad crowd and if Mum didn't leave with me in that moment, we would end up dead and buried out in the Bush. Granddad never messed around, so I took him seriously."

"That's all he said?" Pen questions, but something in his tone catches me off guard.

I sit up and face him. "What's going on? What are you not telling me?"

"I think we should wait for Dom. He can explain better—"

"No, Pen. I want you to explain it to me now. If this is about Brian and my mum, I need to know," I demand, then get up from the bed and start dressing. "Now tell me, please."

"Tell you what?"

I swing around and find Dom standing in the doorway, and he doesn't look happy either.

Chapter Eighteen

D^{om}

"Tell you what?" I grate out. My eyes bounce between a nearly naked Pen, sitting up in bed, and Callum, half-dressed and upset.

"Tell me what you two are hiding from me about Brian," Callum says in a huff as he pulls his t-shirt over his head. "I have every right to know what that bastard has done."

"We aren't—"

Callum raises a hand. "Don't lie to me, Dominic."

Damn it. He's pissed off.

"How about we all get dressed and come out to the living room and talk," I suggest, hoping the bigger space will calm down my irate bassist.

"Fine." Callum stalks past me without looking me in the

eyes. But I see guilt written across his face and I know why. He and Pen slept together, without me.

I glance over to Pen, who looks equally guilty. And he should be, because we've talked about the best way to approach Callum. We should talk with him first about what we want for our future. Talk to him sometime when sex isn't on the table. But apparently, Pen wasn't listening to me.

"You and me, we will be talking about this later," I say, stone-faced.

He lets out a resigned sigh and then mumbles under his breath, "Yeah. Like *we* talk about everything."

Did I just hear him right? I pause for a moment, my eyes narrowing at Pen, the words of denial poised on my lips. But he's right. I haven't been forthcoming about my past—and I can't blame him for being angry.

Therefore, I clamp my mouth shut and leave Pen to get dressed. I head back to the living area, my strides short and my shoulders slumped.

Callum's standing in front of the slider, stiff as a board, and staring out into the darkness of the early morning.

"I never realized just how peaceful this place is," he whispers, but I don't know if it's to himself or me. "Now I know what Danny's been talking about. Maybe finding a piece of property with a lake is better... I need to sell my Evergreen home first." He turns his head and eyes me with an emotion I can't decipher, before returning his attention back to the black of night.

I completely understand—I'd feel the same way. It must be so hard to return to a place where all you see is the shadow of what happened, the weight of that tragedy lingering the moment you walk up to the door. No. I don't blame him for wanting to get rid of the place.

"Come have a seat, Callum," I suggest, but he shakes his head.

I don't push, and remain quiet until Pen comes out. He sits on the end of the sofa and looks to me to start.

"Callum, please sit down," I say, hoping he'll listen this time, but he still doesn't move.

"There's a lot to go over, and I think once you hear what Dom has, you're going to need to sit down," Pen explains.

Callum glances at Pen for a moment, before he nods and sits on the single chair across from him.

So damn stubborn.

"Go on." Callum clasps his hands tightly in his lap, his shoulders hunched inward, eyes fixed on the floor.

"First of all, Pen and I aren't hiding anything from you. Uh-uh-uh, wait," I say as Callum open his mouth to argue. "We wanted to make sure we have all the information before coming to you with details."

"Alright." Still standoffish, Callum is at least looking at me now.

"Let me break it down. First, Dean's guy found out the real reason why your father left Australia."

"*Brian.* And that is?"

"Brian was mixed up with a group that dealt with drugs, prostitution, guns and human trafficking. Pretty much what there is to do illegally, they were—or still may be, doing it."

Callum's eyes go wide. "I remember Granddad saying it was bad, but I didn't know Brian was that corrupt. I wonder if my mum did?"

"Probably. Since Brian was part of the group for the better part of four years until he got caught selling guns to undercover agents. That's when your grandfather got involved and sent you two away."

"Shit." Callum grumbles, rubbing the back of his neck.

"Once this is all done, I need to talk to my mum about keeping secrets."

"Don't blame your mother for not telling you. She was only keeping you safe," Pen says.

"I'm not mad at her. But I wish she had said something to me about it. Then I would have—"

"What would you have done if you knew what you father—sorry, Brian was mixed up in?" I ask, knowing the answer already. He was a kid. There's nothing he could have done—not without repercussions.

Callum sits there, in silence for a long moment, contemplating. "Nothing... I guess."

"Yeah." I give him a second to absorb that, before asking, "Want to hear the rest?"

"Go ahead," he utters solemnly.

"Not long after you and your mom left Australia, Brian made a plea bargain to keep himself out of jail."

"Why am I not surprised," Callum says, his body slumping.

"He turned evidence on the top two men in that organization," I say, watching Callum carefully.

"And now they are after him?" he asks shakily, rubbing at his arms. "Why? After all this time?"

"We don't know, but Dean's tech guy, Levi is digging deep into Brian's current activities."

"And you think they are the ones who are coming after me and my mum?" Callum says, his hands now clenched into fists. "Still, why?"

"I don't know, babe. But until we have solid proof that it's Brian who is bringing this shit to you, we can't ignore anything that comes our way," I explain, lowering myself onto the coffee table to be eye level with him.

"The woman with the gun—what if she—" Callum shutters.

"The woman is in jail. There's no chance she's being let out," I say, hoping the news will give him some sense of comfort and safety.

"She hasn't said who hired her?"

"No. She's tight lipped."

"What about the postman outside my house? Any leads on that?"

"Tobias made some calls—one to Detective Faller and he said he's on it," Pen explains, frustration coating his words.

I'm glad Pen took the lead on that question. I need to focus on Callum so that he doesn't go gonzo and call Brian to bitch him out, exposing what we already know about the shady shit that asshole is currently into.

"Callum." I take his fisted hands into mine and squeeze. "I promise you, Pen and I aren't hiding anything from you. Whatever information we get, we will tell you. But you need to keep a cool head in this."

He nods slowly. "Thanks for explaining it to me." Callum pulls his hands out of mine and stands. "I'm exhausted. I'm going to bed."

Regret filters in, seeing how tired Callum is—not just the lingering pain, but the burden of gloom he's been carrying of this past week.

"See you in the morning," Pen says with a half-hearted smile his way. He wants very much to fall asleep with Callum in his arms. But that's not going to happen—not yet.

There's softness around Pen's eyes when he looks at Callum, like he's trying to be strong even when it's hard to stay away. I too feel the same way, but if we want to make this relationship to work, all three of us need to be on the same page.

As Callum's door quietly closes, Pen straightens in his seat and declares, "Okay, out with it."

"You fucked him," I blurt out. Not so much a question, but an accusation.

"No, I didn't," he defends. "But I'm not surprised that you'd accuse me of that."

"Then what?" I lean toward him, demanding him to be truthful.

"When Callum tells me that he's desperate for my touch, I'm not going to deny him, Dom," Pen declares as he stands and faces off with me. "Or are you angry that you weren't with us?"

"No, I can care less if you two fuck around. I'd watch, but I want to make sure Callum is in this with his heart. Not with his dick only."

"Do you know he's afraid to get into a relationship with us?"

That surprises me. "How do you know that?"

"Because we communicate." He stretches the last word into four syllables and air quotes it, and I get the message. "He started telling me more, until you came into the room and blew things up," Pen jabs, aggravation in his voice.

"Then it is up to us to change that," I say, reaching for Pen. But he steps away, avoiding my touch.

"What now?" Pen utters, avoiding eye contact.

"I'm sorry, baby. I lost my cool and said some stupid shit. Please let me make it up to you." I reach out for him but he still evades my touch. "Come here."

He comes reluctantly, as the frown across his face shows he's debating whether he should or not. But he still won't let me touch him. "I'm still pissed at you."

"I know."

"Do you really?" The hurt is evident in his tone. "We're teetering, Dom. And I'm not sure if I want to stay on."

"I know I have broken your trust, but please believe me, I had no intention to purposely hurt you," I confess, reaching for him again.

Pen releases a breath before he takes my hand and slowly walks to me.

"Please don't get mad for asking, but if you didn't fuck our guy, then what did you with him?"

His frown slowly disappears, and a small smile slides across his handsome face. "Sucked off his sweet cock. Want a taste? I know you're yearning to taste him again."

A hint of jealousy blooms in my chest—not because he tasted Callum, but because of the truthful taunt Pen is dangling in front of me. I've been yearning to be inside Callum again. To taste his flavor on my tongue—share him with the only other man in my life.

But if Pen wants to play that way, I'm game. I don't give Pen time to react as I launch myself at him, gripping the back of his neck and slamming my mouth over his. I go all in with tongue and teeth, biting his lips.

He grunts before opening up wider for me and I shove my tongue farther into his mouth. If I could, I'd dip deeper down his throat and try to taste what's left of Callum's essence.

"Fuck... Dom," Pen croons as my left hand tightens around the back of his neck and I draw his body tight to mine.

"That's exactly what we're going to do. Unbutton your pants and drop them," I order. Pen quickly does my bidding, while I do the same.

I spin Pen around, grip his hair at the nape and push him forward until he's bent over the sofa. I follow him down, brushing my aching dick against his smooth ass. I hiss in pleasure. "Now, while I fuck you, you're going to stay quiet. Not a sound, will come out of your mouth. Hear me?"

Pen nods in eager understanding. He loves when I get rough with him, taking him hard with only the heavy slick of precum from my uncut cock. And lucky for him, I'm one of those men that makes a lot precum.

A light creak to my left tells me that Callum's not sleeping. In fact, I suspect he's watching us, which amps up my lust and the need to fuck Pen fast and deep so I can get both men off at the same time.

Pen softly groans, drawing my attention back to him. "I told you to keep quiet." I slap his ass hard, leaving a handprint for him to admire later, and then grind my dick against his crease.

He pushes his ass against me as his breathing hitches. He's desperate for more contact and I'm going to give it to him.

"Spit," I command, putting my hand to Pen's mouth. He sucks on my fingers first before he spits on them.

I move my hand to his pucker and rub his saliva around as I jerk my cock until precum dribbles from the tip. I remove my hand and put my thick mushroom head to his hole and thoroughly coat his entrance.

Then I grip his shoulder with one hand and use my other to guide my tip in until I push past the first ring of muscle. I pause, taking a breath, and I feel Pen's body relaxing under my touch.

After giving him a second or two more to adjust, I slowly and carefully glide my steely pole inside his tight heat until my balls are plastered to his ass.

Pen turns his head, meeting my eyes with hungry passion. He bites his lower lip and closes his eyes, a silent plea for me to move. His silent request instantly heats up my already explosive need to drive in deep and come inside Pen.

My leisurely thrusts are gone, replaced with powerful thrusts at a frantic pace.

"Fuck, baby—yes," I utter as I move to grip his shoulders with both hands, never losing my rhythm. Over and over, I plow into his ass until I feel the sensation of need in my balls.

A soft groan to my left has me smiling wide. Callum is also getting off as he's watching us. I imagine him with his pants down around his thighs while he slides his beautiful cock through his tight fist. That image of him amps up my explosive desire and I begin to piston harder and faster in and out of Pen's hole.

The feel of Pen's ass tightening around my cock brings me to the edge. The demand to drive even harder inside him wins. There's no time for more rough play. No time to make this fucking last longer. With Callum watching us like a voyeur, and Pen bent over for me, I grit my teeth tight and shoot my load inside him.

My ears catch Callum's soft hiss and with Pen's muffled whimper, I know they are coming too.

I eventually hunch forward, leaning heavily on Pen's slumped over form.

"So good," Pen utters under his breath. "Now get off me before I fall over."

I straighten and see Pen's cum sliding down the back of the sofa. Thank Christ, the sofa is leather. It'll be easy to clean up, or Tobias—no, Danny will tear into us for soiling his favorite piece of furniture.

I slap Pen's ass once more and say, "Let's clean up and go to bed. Tomorrow, we'll talk."

I grab paper towels and a spray cleaner while Pen rolls his eyes before heading to the bathroom. I watch him disappear inside, but in my periphery, I catch sight of the door to Callum's room silently closing. Damn, I was hoping to see his face. To see the flushed, just-come expression in his eyes.

His action proves that Callum is ours. And no amount of denial from him is going to make me think otherwise. And I'm going to tell him so, tomorrow.

I rake my fingers through my hair in frustration. In a perfect world, expressing my feelings should come easy. But it's not—it's the complete opposite of easy for me. However, I *have* to try, since Callum and Pen are the two most important people in my life.

After Pen leaves the bathroom, I head in. I pull my phone from my jeans pocket and the movement wakes it up. On my lock screen is a notification of a missed call.

Jesus, I was so caught up with being inside Pen that I didn't hear my phone ring.

When I open the app and listen to the message that was left, shock rolls through me at the familiar voice. It's Gregory Joust, my old boss from the U.S. Marshals office.

It's been fourteen years since I last saw that son of a bitch —on the day he canned me. And now he's demanding that I come in because he has important information that I need to know? But then he drops a code word that nearly causes me to throw my phone at the wall.

Fuck that.

Instead of reaching out to Greg, I call Tobias. He'll give me his opinion on how to proceed with this message. Despite my plan, I have a sinking feeling I'm going on a plane ride.

Chapter Nineteen

P^{en}

I wake up slowly, my vision blurry. Rubbing at my eyes until it clears, I see the clock radio. It displays seven fifteen in the morning.

Jesus, I overslept.

I slowly move from my side to my back and feel every glorious twinge in my sore ass. Dom fucked me good last night, but I'm not complaining. I love the domineering side of my boyfriend. Lately though, it seems like during sex is the only time I get to see the real Dom. Not the one who's hiding his past.

Why can't I let that go? If Dom doesn't want to talk about his past, then I need to respect that—and stop asking him. Still, it bugs me that he has secrets he's not willing to share with me when I basically opened a vein of my life for the man.

Shake it off damn it. You love him and that's all that matters.

Focusing on the love we share, I yawn as I reach over to my right to find that side of the bed empty. And cold.

I should expect his absence. Dom's always up before me. As much as I would like to lay in bed all morning, I have a routine to follow, and Callum to protect.

I get up, go take a piss and then look in on Callum. With him still sound asleep, I jump into the shower. Lathering myself up, I think back to last night. Getting Callum off with my mouth was epic. Then getting fucked by Dom. It was a very good night.

A surge of lust begins to pool heavy in my balls. I squirt some bodywash into my hands and start stroking my cock vigorously until I come with a silent moan. Then I rinse off and get out of the shower.

After getting dressed, I walk into the large, open concept living space expecting to see Dom waiting for me in the kitchen. Yet, the room is empty. My partner is nowhere in sight and he hasn't started his usual morning routine—the coffee maker isn't on, nor has he set out our food like he usually does.

"Where the heck are you?" I look through the glass slider, assuming Dom might be out on the deck, enjoying the water view. But he isn't out there either.

As I take a step outside to make sure, my phone vibrates with a call. Not wanting to wake Callum, I continue onto the deck and glance at the screen. It's Ron.

That's strange.

I tap to accept. "Good morning. This is a bit early for you," I greet Warrior Black's former manager.

"Yes, it is," he says, his voice slightly shaky. "But since you didn't call me last week, *Pennington*, I figured I should call to ask if everything's okay with you." The saucy way Ron says my full name tells me he's upset. He knows I despise hearing it. My mother used to call me that when I was in trouble.

I've been calling Ron almost daily since he announced his colon cancer diagnosis, just to make sure he's doing okay. Who could blame me when this man did so much for me when my parents practically disowned me when I came out.

But my mind has been so focused on Callum's attack and everything else that has happened, I haven't stopped to think of Ron.

Guilt churns in my gut. "I'm sorry. There has been—"

"I know. Dean has been filling me in on what's been happening. And I'm the one who's sorry. I don't mean to make you feel guilty for not calling me. I just want to make sure you're okay."

"I am... Wait a second." *Are those beeping sounds in the background?* "Are you at your chemo treatment today?"

"Yes. The center couldn't fit me in for a later time," he explains evenly. "Don't worry, though. I'm not dying... Yet."

"Ron," I growl, not liking how he jokes about his death.

"Pen," he mock-huffs, trying to sound like me.

I chuckle. "Who's with you?"

"Dean, as usual. He's getting some coffee right now," he says, then lets out a small cough.

My spine snaps straight. "Are you sick? Did you tell the doctor about your cough?"

"Jesus, boy. Calm your jets. It's only a cough," he says haughtily. "Now, the reason why I'm calling you—and don't get mad at me, but I've been talking to your mother."

It's like a boulder landed square on my chest at his announcement. "Why?"

"Because she's your family. And you need your family, Pen."

"You didn't," I counter, feeling slightly betrayed. My temper begins to simmer. "I don't need family like that, Ron."

"Everyone needs family, so don't argue with me."

I rake a hand through my hair in frustration and swallow hard. "What did you two talk about?"

"You."

I shake my head. "I get that. What else?"

He lets out a loud sigh. "Your mother loves you and wants to talk—wants to understand."

"There's nothing to understand. She is just frustrated because I won't listen to *her* reasons," I say, feeling a headache coming on.

"She wants to understand why you won't answer her calls or call her back and talk to her," Ron further explains.

"That's it?" I say, slightly surprised. I expected Ron to relay back one of my mother's passages from the Bible. She's good at selectively quoting from it.

"Yes. She just misses you and wants to talk. Now tell me, why aren't you picking up her calls?"

"Because I don't want to hear her righteous sermons about how being gay is a sin. I'm done with it, Ron," I convey, as an ache creeps up into my throat, partially strangling me.

While I lived at home, I was spoon fed Catholic pabulum until I was choking on it. Now that I'm free and out of my parents' household, I can truly be me. I don't have to worry about who I offend with my sexuality.

"Pen. Listen to me. Life is too short. I know this. And if my parents were still alive, I'd try—I would. I'd try and try to get them to remember the love they had for me. But that isn't possible for me now. For you, it is. Since your mother is willing to talk, take the chance and maybe you can heal your relationship, and she can grow. Promise me you'll do this."

I can't believe he's asking me to shred my reticence and take the leap. My parents aren't willing, so why should I be? "And if she goes back to the way she's been with me?"

"Well, that is up to her. But I feel you need to give her another chance, Pen," he says before he starts coughing again—harder this time.

"Are you alright, Ron?" I ask as my pulse escalates into a full gallop.

"Babe, sit back. Here's some water." I hear Dean's voice and I'm quickly relieved that Ron isn't alone. "Pen?"

"Yeah, Dean?"

"Ron needs rest right now. Can he call you later?" Dean's rigid tone gives me no room to argue.

"Yeah, yeah. Give him a hug for me," I say, as I try to swallow the large knot forming at the base of my throat, but the ache intensifies. Ever since Ron was diagnosed with cancer, I've been on pins and needles worrying about my friend. "Tell him I will try the next time my mother calls."

"Umm... Okay, I will," Dean says before hanging up.

I stand there for a moment, absorbing what wasn't said. By Dean or by Ron.

Is Ron sicker than he's letting on? With every phone call before this one, he has sounded good and strong. But is he just that good at hiding how sick he really is? And I can't believe I agreed to talk to my mother.

"Pen."

I swivel my head in the direction of the driveway, where Fig and Jordan are walking toward me. "What's up?" I say, sliding the phone into my back pocket.

"Is everything all right?" Fig asks with concern.

"Yeah, why?"

"You look upset," Jordan adds. "Did you hear from Dom?"

"Dom?" I frown. "What do you mean?"

They look at each other before Figs says, "Dom left early this morning. Didn't he tell you?"

"What?" Dom left. And again, he didn't tell me he was leaving. "Where did he go?"

"We don't know." Fig shrugs. "All he said is that he'll be back as soon as possible."

"He didn't say anything else?" I ask, anger clawing at my new-found confidence in our relationship. I can't believe he's done it again. They shake their heads. "Thanks."

I walk away from them and head back inside the house, feeling like my heart is shattering into a million pieces. We were supposed to talk today. Smooth out the wrinkles in our relationship. But here he goes and leaves without a word to me. Again. It's not like I wasn't sleeping right fucking next to him. He will probably use the excuse of not wanting to wake me, but that's bullshit.

I'm done. I can't be in a relationship with a partner who can't see and trust me.

"Pen? What's wrong?" Callum is in my space, eyes wide with worry.

The red haze in my thoughts clears as I look at the beautiful man before me. A poison dart of pain shoots down to my soul, knowing that I have to tell him that this throuple Dom and I proposed to him isn't happening.

"Where's Dom?"

"I don't fucking know where he went," I say, venom seeping into my words and I immediately regret it. "I'm sorry."

He leans in, cups my face with both hands. "Tell me, what's going on between you and Dom."

I step away from his touch to give myself room to breathe, even though Callum is my solace. "I don't know if I can do this anymore."

"What can't you do?" he asks, but remains where he is to give me the space I need.

"Between Dom and me. He doesn't trust me and today proves it," I admit, trying to keep the dam holding back my emotions from bursting.

I can't cry.

"I don't understand. What happened today to make you rethink your relationship with him?"

"He keeps secrets from me, and I'm tired of always asking about what or who or even how in his life, and him never answering. I'm sorry, but I thought the three of us could make it work and I now know it can't." The strangled feeling around my neck gets tighter as I finally admit my feelings for Callum. "I love you, but I can't do it anymore." I walk out of the house, hoping he doesn't follow me.

"Pen," Callum calls after me, but I go from striding to a full out run.

I pass Fig and Jordan and tell them to watch over Callum while I go for a run. And without waiting for their agreement, I take off down the small trail I found a few days ago.

The rough terrain isn't enough to take my mind off of what I just did. I broke up with Callum—even before he agreed to be with us. And I inadvertently splintered any relationship he might have with Dom without him being present.

I'm such a loser.

It's taking everything in me not to drive out of this place and redo my life without him. Without his secrets. Hide myself away from the world until I know what I want. Hide away from Dom so he can't find me and sweet talk my fractured heart into forgiving him yet again. Because if I have to go through this one more time, my heart will combust and burn into ashes from the hurt.

Chapter Twenty

The last place I expected to be this morning was in a hallway of the United States Department of Justice building in Virginia, yet here I am. I was once a Deputy Marshal GS-9, and I've walked these halls an umpteenth number of times. I should be comfortable here. But I'm not. I have been battling PTSD since the last case I was on—a case that went horribly wrong, and being here is making my skin crawl.

Twitchy and unbalanced is how I'm feeling as I stand around here like an idiot waiting for someone to take me to see my old boss. Deputy Director Gregory Joust.

When Greg called late last night and left a voicemail with the old code word, X-Acto, my entire body locked up and my mind whirled back to the last time I saw the son of a bitch who fired me.

There has been only one other time that code was used. Over fourteen years ago on the day a witness lost his life and my partner Rick's and my lives were irrevocably changed.

Rick and I were protecting a witness who'd agreed to testify against a major crime syndicate. The witness, Jacob Cunningham, ended up murdered, Rick was almost killed, and I took a bullet in my shoulder and another one in my left hip—and was accused of divulging the location of the safe house where we'd stashed the witness. The whole case was built on that witness's testimony, and with him dead, there was nothing. As far as I know, they never found out who leaked the location, but I know for damn sure it wasn't me.

In the end, I lost more than some small pieces of flesh and a job. I lost my dignity, my livelihood, the people who I thought were my friends, and the life I had built in DC. They stripped me of my rank and then fired me. After four months of having my every move watched, they concluded that I was innocent of all of the accusations and cleared of all charges. I didn't get my job back, though, and my reputation was mud by that point.

Those were dark days for me. I drank and drank until I didn't know which way was up or if I was pissing down. It brought me to the lowest point in my life, and it took nearly a full year for Dean to pull my sorry ass out of the epic hole I had shoveled myself into.

Standing here now brings back the old urge to pick up a bottle and drink until my mind becomes nothing but fog and mush. But then I think of Pen—my beautiful Pen. Smart, energetic and honest. And Callum. He's sweet and gentle, and all too giving. I think of them and I'm able to drive away the urge to drink—the urge to put myself back in that hole again.

"Mr. Rossetti?" A female voice pulls me out of my dour thoughts.

A pretty brunette approaches me. Her dark blue suit is cut to perfection and highlights her full, curvy figure, but the stoney expression on her face tells me all I need to know about her. "I'm Agent Donna Waldon. Please follow me," she says icily. She doesn't extend a hand, and I'm not surprised by it. I don't peg her as a U.S. marshal—too stiff in her manner. Bet she's FBI, because her less-than-friendly demeanor fits that profile to a tee.

Now why would an FBI agent be present in the U.S. Marshal's office?

"Why was I called here, Agent Waldon? And why is the FBI involved?" I ask, not hiding my irritation.

She abruptly turns, surprise written all over her face before her indifference slams down like a steel door. "Deputy Director Greg Joust will tell you everything you need to know," she says without answering any of my questions.

Jesus. Her stone-cold manner is no help as I try to gauge how serious a situation I'm walking into. I let out a quiet huff, and follow the woman through a set of double doors, where I walk into a den of vipers.

The moment I step into the outer office area with all its cubicles and desks, conversations taper off as marshals that once used to be my friends have shock written across their faces. Other, less familiar, marshals exhibit disgust or simple disdain in their eyes. No one approaches me. Now why would I expect them to act any differently?

Do they still see guilt across my face?

A door ahead of me opens and out walks Joust. Definitely older, but his sharp, eagle-eye stare hasn't changed. He still reminds me of a riled-up badger. Mostly bluster, but watch out for his teeth because he has a vicious bite.

"Mr. Rossetti," he says sternly. Again, no handshake, but I'm not expecting it from him either. This isn't a friendly visit.

"Joust," I reply and step past the threshold into his office.

Donna walks in after me, and Joust closes the door. If she's in on this, then something big is coming down. But what? I'm afraid to ask.

"Have a seat, Rossetti," Joust says, pointing to the black chair adjacent to his desk.

"No thanks. Now tell me why I'm here," I demand, my tone less than pleasant.

Joust's eyes narrow before he takes his own seat. He motions toward Agent Waldon. "Agent Waldon is the chief analyst for the Federal Bureau of Investigation. I'm sure she introduced herself."

I slice a glance at her before turning my attention back to Joust. "Just barely. Now answer the question. Why am I here?"

"A situation was brought to our attention about five months ago." Greg shuffles papers around on his desk, then picks up a folder and hands it to me.

"What is it?" I nod toward the folder but don't reach for it.

"Everything you want to know is in here," he says and extends his arm out further. "Take it."

My eyes slice to the female fed, and then to the folder, before I grab it and sit. I open the flap and the first thing I see is a picture of the body of a black man, and then I notice the bullet wound in the center of his forehead. Examining the photo, something snags my memory, but not enough to jog it. "Execution style. Hmm... Who is this?"

Joust's eyes shift to Donna, who moves into my line of sight. "That's Mangrove Gilbert, he was one of our planted agents, pretending to be a small-time dealer so he could infiltrate the Trendoya gang and find out who's been supplying large amounts of fentanyl to them. Manny has been building up evidence to take down the drug supplier through this group. But the last time we heard from him was six weeks ago, when he sent a message that he had a lead. He was due in court next week on an unrelated case, to testify against one of the leaders of an affiliate gang. But as you can see now, Manny's dead," she explains.

"His body was found yesterday at a truck stop off of I-70, just outside of Grand Junction, Colorado," Joust explains further.

That's not far from Evergreen—we drove through there four days ago. *Could it be a coincidence? I fucking hope so.* "What does this have to do with me?" I glance at the photos of the dead agent again and something sparks in my mind. It is almost reminiscent of...

Joust shifts in his chair, drawing my attention. He opens his desk drawer and takes out four more folders. "These are similar," he says as he hands them to me. "They all were killed the same way."

"Again. What does this have to do with me?" My eyes remain fixed on Joust. The way the man barely moves in his seat, I know he's hiding something. Even though it's been years, I've been around and worked with this man too many times to forget his tells.

I totally ignore the folders and the fed next to me. "I'm no longer a marshal—haven't been in a long time. But I know there's something you aren't telling me. Either spill, or I'm out of here," I declare, anger seeping out with my words.

Donna speaks up. "We think whoever is killing our agents is following the pattern from the Jacob Cunningham case."

"And?" I snap, glaring at her. I'm tired of their games.

"We think they are going to come after you next," Joust announces as he stands.

"What?" That's the last thing I expected him to say.

"We think the killer who shot Jacob Cunningham is back. Our intel says the Mastov family wants every witness to that event eliminated."

"That simply doesn't make any sense," I admit, then think about my ex-partner. "What about Rick?"

"We sent him a message asking him to also show today, but he never got back to us," Donna explains.

"I saw him a few days ago," I say, not wanting to give details, but if what they say is true, then he's also in trouble. "He called me asking for help. Someone jumped him and he thinks people are following him everywhere he goes."

"We'll get a man on him," Joust announces, picking up the phone.

I open the rest of the folders. Four men and a woman. All killed the same way.

"These were my agents, who were, at some point, part of that case you were involved in," she admits, pointing to the men.

"And the woman?"

"A partner, who we guess was there at the time and got caught up."

Shit. Then a thought hits me and I look at Donna. "Do you think whoever is doing this might go after people associated with me, too?"

Donna Waldon doesn't pause. "I wouldn't put it past the killer to go after anyone near their target until they get to the one they want."

That isn't what I want to hear. Then something else hits me. "There's no way. I would have known these men," I say, trying to piece together what Waldon and Joust just told me with my memories of that case. "Mangrove." I glance down at the folder. "He and one other were supposed to take the next shift to watch Jacob, but they never showed up—am I correct?"

"Yes. They were held up by traffic." Her tone suggests otherwise.

"But you don't believe that, do you?" I push, because I didn't believe it back then either.

"I don't know what to believe," she finally admits. There's a small tick in her right eye, which tells me she's lying.

"Jesus Christ, you think Rick and I were also part of the set up—You can't deny it—I see it in your eyes," I say with absolute confidence as she shakes her head.

"Rossetti." Joust's lips are pinched thin, but I don't stop with my own interrogation.

"You think they were paid off to stay away," I accuse, as the pieces click into place like the tumblers in a lock. "Both Rick and I were supposed to die, but we didn't because the gunshots to my body were superficial, but Rick's..." Yes, this has to be what that was. "You think we were a part of the plan the Mastov family set up."

"Don't put words in my mouth," Waldon snaps out like a whip.

"Rossetti," Joust says, a lot less tension in his voice. "We are not accusing you of the set up."

The more I think about that day, the more my revelation solidifies. "Sure as hell sounds like she is."

"We just want you to be aware of what happened and take precautionary measures," Joust says evenly.

"You know we didn't have to tell you anything about this case or the circumstances, but Joust felt obliged," Donna says with a bit of grit in her tone.

"Good to know," I say right back to her, not giving a fuck what she thinks, and turn back to Joust. "That old case ruined my career, nearly pinned me with Jacob's murder and implicated me as the narc of the crime family. I have no inclination to play nice with either of you."

"Come on now, Dominic. Let's all be civil," Joust says earnestly.

Well, that's new. I have never before heard my first name come out of that man's mouth. If there's truth behind what he and the fed are saying, then there's a chance the killer is after me—and that sends my worry factor into the stratosphere. The band—especially Callum, and Pen... Everyone's lives are in danger. I need to get the hell out of here and call Tobias and Dean.

Chapter Twenty-One

allum

"Where's Pen?" I interrupt Jordan as he and Joel are talking to another one of Dean's men in the driveway.

"Last I saw him, he was running toward the trails," Jordan says, pointing in the direction of the woods. "Do you need me to radio him to come back?"

"No. I'll go find him."

"I'm not sure if that's a good idea, you walking alone in the woods. Let one of us go with you," Jordan says.

"I don't need a babysitter while I'm here, do I?" I ask, doubtful that I need a bodyguard. Pen can't be that far off.

"Yes, you do. I promised Pen I'd keep an eye on you and I'm not going back on my word. I'm coming with you."

"Fine," I huff and begin walking toward the narrow trail

up ahead. "But if Pen and I need space to talk, then you're gone."

"Got it," Jordan salutes and follows behind me.

Even though I'm anxious while looking for Pen, the walk through the woods is refreshing. Spring is in full bloom, but the air still has a little bite to it—it's like a sweet Honeycrisp apple. Buying property similar to this has been at the back of my mind since we got here, and the farther I walk through the California wilderness, the idea begins to feel more like my new reality.

"Where the heck is he?" I ask over my shoulder to Jordan —except he's not there. I turn back around and scan the area. "Jordan," I shout, but I don't see or even hear him.

Then all the hairs on the back of my neck rise, and my skin becomes gooseflesh. My instinct is telling me to run like the devil is chasing me, but in which direction? Back to where I came from? Or do I keep moving ahead and shout for Pen? And am I healed enough to even run very far?

I check my pockets. "Damn it." I forgot my cell phone on the kitchen table.

A crack of what I think is a branch being stepped on has me freezing in place. Then I hear another. I take off in the direction I was walking, but I haven't been on this path before and soon realize that it doesn't lead to the other side of the lake. No—it leads to a small open field.

I'm exposed, and panic seizes my brain. I can't think. Then I hear my name being called. "Callum."

Overcome with relief, I'm about to respond... except that the relief allows me to think again. There is a creep factor to the man's tone that has fear gripping my chest to the point that I'm losing my breath.

"Callum." The lyrical tone triggers a memory. A memory

that dredges up terror. All the air leaves my lungs, because I know exactly who this is.

Oh god. It's him.

I blindly take off toward the security of dense trees on the opposite side of the clearing. Low branches scratch at my face and arms as I run through them. Stinging pain along my cheeks doesn't deter me from racing away from that bastard. Neither does the pain in my arm after I smack my splint on a sapling when I stumble against it.

As I pass through a more heavily wooded area, my hair feels like its being pulled. I swear the trees are alive and grabbing for me.

Just keep running, I can hear Granddad say in my head. Or am I becoming delusional?

"Callum!"

I hear my name again, but this time, my heart eases back from the terror. "Pen!"

"Keep calling for me, Callum," I hear him shout from a distance.

I pause for a moment, trying to calm my racing heart. The pounding in my ears is making it impossible to gauge which direction Pen is shouting from. "Pen!"

"I'm here," he responds back, his voice getting louder. "Don't move. Just call my name."

"Pen," I shout again. As I keep scanning my surroundings, I am filled with an eerie certainty that someone is watching me. And was I hearing Pen calling my name from afar? Or was it my attacker?

"Callum." Pen's close, I can hear him up ahead. As I start to walk in that direction, pain explodes from the back of my head and my vision goes dark.

"Callum. Sweetheart. Wake up for me." I can hear Pen's voice, but the pain behind my eyes is making it difficult to open them. "Christ sakes, why isn't my radio working?"

"Pen?" I say in a whisper. "What happened?"

"I don't know, babe. But I found you out cold, on the ground. Did you trip and hit your head?" Pen has my head propped on his lap and is gently checking my scalp. "You do have a bump on the back of your skull. Let me look in your eyes."

"What?" I say, finally opening my lids and looking up at Pen's worried gaze.

"You're coming off one concussion and you just got another knock on the head." He studies my eyes for a minute. "Your pupils look fine. Am I blurry?"

"No. You always look fine, Pen," I say with a slight smile.

Pen kisses my forehead. "I think you're all right. So back to business. Why are you walking alone in the woods? I thought I told—"

"Jordan was with me, then suddenly he was gone. Then I heard... *his* voice—but I think maybe it was you calling me, and I just thought it was him because I was panicked and alone. But I can't be sure," I confess, trying to sit up.

"Move slow. I want you to get your bearings before you get to your feet."

"Pen. I swear it," gripping his hand tightly. "Something actually hit the back of my head because I felt pain before I blacked out," I explain, trying to rehash the event in my mind.

"You said *his voice*. Who were you referring to? Do you think it was Jordan calling for you?" Pen asks as he helps me to sit up.

I meet his stare with a note of apprehension. I don't want him to think I'm losing it. "No, it wasn't Jordan. Pen, it was my attacker. I swear it sounded just like him. But maybe—"

"Don't doubt yourself. We can't discount anything right now," Pen says as he grasps both my hands and slowly hauls me to my feet. "Are you able to walk on your own?"

I take a calming breath, then a step to make sure I won't get dizzy. "I'm good, for now."

"Okay. Now where were you when you heard his voice?"

I lead Pen back in the direction I came from... hopefully. When we arrive at the clearing, I point to where the voice seemed to come from.

"I hope Jordan isn't hurt like I was," I say, slowly scanning the area. "This is where he should have been when I heard him."

"When was the last time you *saw* Jordan?" Pen asks as he studies the ground around us.

"Not much farther," I say and start walking in the direction.

"Don't move," he says and I freeze on the spot.

Pen carefully walks over to me, his eyes focused on the ground. He bends down and studies a print in the soil.

"What did you find?"

"Not sure yet. But," he pulls out his cell phone and takes a picture of the shoe print. Then he proceeds to reach for some sticks and carefully surrounds the print with them. I don't ask what he's doing since it's self-explanatory. "Let's go find Jordan."

He takes my hand and we walk back until we find the trail I started on. But there's no Jordan.

Pen's radio chirps. "Come in, Pen. Fig here."

He taps his earpiece. "Is Jordan with you?"

"That's a no. I was told that he went with Callum to look for you."

"Yes, but I found Callum alone, and hurt. Gather Joel and Dean's men and meet us where the trail meets the gravel drive."

"Ten-four."

"Pen." I swallow down the worry and ask, "Where's Dom?"

"I don't fucking know. Right now, he's not my concern. You are," he says with some bite, but I know his anger isn't aimed at me.

I just hope that Dom gets back here soon to help find Jordan and track down whoever is on the property. I won't be able to sleep otherwise. And while I believe Dom can help find Jordan and figure out what just happened to me, I'm not sure he can fix his relationship with Pen. I don't know what I was thinking about, wanting to be in a relationship with these men.

This only proves my thinking about relationships. They never work.

Chapter Twenty-Two

P^{en}

I lead Callum along the trail to the gravel drive, which is about a click away from the house. Fig and the guys meet up with us, and I tell them what happened to Callum. Then we quickly decide to dispatch men in different directions to find Jordan.

When I get my hands on him, we aren't just having words. Before I kick his sorry untrustworthy ass off our team, we are going rounds for endangering Callum.

I remain with Callum as we head to the house, even though I can already see that he's distancing himself from me. There's a gap between us—it's small, but it could be the Grand Canyon for all the space and silence he's keeping.

Maybe this is for the better. Since I'm done with Dom, I don't feel right continuing on with Callum. The way he's avoiding eye contact, he appears to be thinking the same thing.

Even so, all this could have been avoided if I had stayed put and not run away to lick my wounds.

I decide that I can't worry about what's going through Callum's head right now. His safety is what's most important.

"Pen," Callum says as we enter the house, but I keep quiet. "Where are you?"

"Thinking."

"About what?" I don't respond. He grips my shoulder, and turns me toward him and repeats his question. "About what?"

I glance his way, but I can't really look at him—not with those scratches still marring his skin, yellow-green and fading, reminders of how close I came to losing him. "You've already been through enough, and if I hadn't taken off on you, you wouldn't have left the house."

His grip on my shoulder tightens and he gets in my face. "Now you listen to me. This is *not* your fault. Do you hear me?" He peers into my eyes and I see so much strength in them. I want to wrap my arms around this man and protect him from the world. But I can see he wouldn't want that. He gives me a little shake. "Answer me, asshole."

"Yes," I chuckle, even though I don't feel any happiness— not like I did last night.

"Usually, I'm more than capable of taking care of myself, but apparently, right now I'm not. So, I propose, once this whole thing is cleared up, you teach me some moves to protect myself. What do you think?"

"Yes, I can do that," I agree, if only to cement his sense of purpose. Whether or not I stick around once we find the bastard who's behind this... well, we'll deal with that later.

"I'm going to clean up. I want to be part of the conversation you have with the team once they get back."

"Take your time and don't rush." I watch Callum go into his bedroom and close the door. I'm not sure if I want him involved in this conversation with the team. But the only people here that I currently trust are Fig. I need to talk to him now.

I step outside and find all but one man pulling up near the front door. "Did you locate Jordan?"

"We couldn't find him," Joel says. His brows are furrowed tight and he's frowning just like the rest of the group. "Jordan's absence is suspect to me."

Me too.

Fig arrives with George by his side; both are shaking their heads. "Couldn't track him," Fig admits.

I turn to Dean's men. "How well do you know Jordan?" I'm nowhere near calm.

"We don't know him at all," Patch says.

"I met him in Colorado, when Dean sent us there," Pete adds, with an equal amount of confusion across his face.

"We thought he was part of *your* crew," Joel says confidently. "He told us back in Evergreen that he's been a part of your group for a year."

"That's true," Fig adds. "He did start with us when all that crap happened with Connor's uncle."

A chill runs down my spine. "I only met him when he was assigned to Warrior Black," I explain, then pull out my phone and quickly dial Tobias's number.

"Pen."

"How did Jordan come to us?" I ask, putting my phone on speaker and turning up the volume so everyone can hear.

Right then, Callum comes out, stands by me and listens

attentively to Tobias. "He came to us from Dean Harper's crew last year. Why?"

"Dean's men confirm that they never met Jordan until they got to Colorado," I state, gripping the phone tight.

"Fuck," Tobias hisses. "Are you sure?"

"Yes. And there's more."

"What?" he clips out, an edge of ire coating the word.

"Callum was spooked in the woods. He thought he heard the same man who attacked him in Evergreen call out his name here. Then he got knocked out. He has a large lump on the back of his head."

"I need to call Dean. Wait for my call back."

"Wait," I begin to say, but he hangs up. I wanted to ask if he had heard from Dom.

"What do we do in the mean time?" Fig asks, as he looks to me.

I glance at Callum, and the storm of emotions across his face gives me no choice but to propose that we get the hell out of here. "Since this place isn't any safer than Colorado, we are heading to San Francisco. And you, Callum Fitz, will be under lock and key until all this is over."

Chapter Twenty-Three

As I clip on my lap belt in the private jet Dean procured for me, my phone vibrates with a call. I pick it up, glance at the screen and release a breath before tapping *Accept*.

"Thanks for picking up the call," Leo says with a chuckle.

"You are welcome. Now tell me what you got. Is Callum's mom safe? Did you find the person who's been fucking with Rick?"

"Callum's mom is all set. But Rick... I tried calling Rick after you reached out to me, but he never answered. I even tried to text him, thinking he's afraid to answer an unknown number, but I never got a response back. So..."

"That's odd. I'll call him once I get off with you," I say.

"You know I don't play that way, Rossetti," Leo replies with another laugh.

"You wish," I counter, then see that I have another call coming in. "Hey, gotta go. But I'll call you later about Rick."

"Sounds good." Then Leo hangs up, and I answer the other call.

"What the hell, Dom? I don't appreciate your cryptic message to call you back," Tobias growls.

"Sorry, man. But you didn't pick up earlier and I didn't want to talk until I got on the plane. We have a problem. I don't think the attacks on Callum are from Brian."

"What do you mean?"

"Not going into details, but you know I used to be a U.S. Marshal. One of my past cases might have caught up with me."

"I need full disclosure, Dom," Tobias demands.

"Can we do this when I—"

"There's a change in plans," Tobias interjects. "You're coming straight to San Fran. Dean's guys are already filing a new flight plan for your plane."

"No. I have to get back to Bear—"

"Callum was attacked again. So everyone is coming here."

"Callum was attacked? Is he hurt?"

"Someone smashed him in the back of his skull."

Shock and rage rips through me. My insides are shredded. I wasn't there to protect Callum. Even with Pen and the rest of the security team surrounding Callum, he still got hurt.

"There's something else," Tobias's tone snaps me out of my head. I'm paying full attention.

"What is it?"

"Pen thinks Jordan might be part of this."

"How? Dean wouldn't have sent someone to us if they were—"

"That's the crook. Dean didn't send him."

I don't know what to say to that admission.

"I want this finished, Dom. Got me?" He barks out the two words, which has my back going ramrod stiff.

"You and me both," I say, evenly through my teeth. I'm not mad at Tobias, only the situation we are in.

"We will see you in about seven hours." Then he hangs up. Jesus, I can't stand when he does that. But I hate this situation even more.

Instead of waiting, I dial Pen's number. I need the details on why Pen thinks Jordan is involved. And where the fuck was he, when all this shit took place.

I let the call go until Pen's voicemail announces that there's no more room. Since he didn't pick up, I call Callum.

"Dom, where the fuck are you?" His urgent tone is near volatile.

"Are you okay?" I ask calmly. Getting riled won't do either of us any good.

"Am I okay?" Callum huffs. "Yes, I'm okay. Pen's helping me with my anxieties."

"Tobias told me what happened. Where were you when you got attacked?" Silence. "Callum?"

"I was looking for Pen. After he found out you left without letting us know anything, he got pissed and needed time. He went for a run in the woods. Since I didn't want him to be alone, I went looking for him with Jordan as my security. Then Jordan disappeared and I heard my name called. At first, I thought it was Pen. But when my name was called again, I knew it was my attacker."

"And that whole time, you were alone... In the woods," I growl. "Pen—"

"This isn't Pen's fault. It's yours," he says straight up.

As I open my mouth to refute his accusation, I realize

Callum might be correct. I left right after I got the message from Joust. Right after I'd been balls deep into Pen. I just left without a word. I had promised Pen that I'd keep him in the loop but I broke my pact with him by not waking him up and telling him what was happening.

"You're right," I finally say, filled with guilt. I broke Pen's trust and for that, he might break what we have. "How is he?"

"I don't know. He's in fucking hulk protection mode. He won't talk to me and I blame this all on you." The hurt behind his words is equally sharp and it is digging deep into my heart.

"I'm sorry. I'll fix it between us."

"You've said that before, and I don't believe you, Dom. And neither does Pen. That's why he didn't answer his phone."

"I guessed that. Listen, I'm on a plane getting ready to take off to San Fran. I'll fix this between Pen and I. Then we three need to talk, after we track down the bastard behind this," I say, not wanting to explain further.

Callum remains silent, and I can hear what he's not saying. He, too, is giving up on us, and I can't have that.

"Listen to me, this is the most honest and open thing I'm going to say to you."

"And what is that?" There's a clear note of resistance in his voice.

"I love you, Callum. And tell Pen I love him too. And I'm not giving up on us. No matter what."

"Dom," he says with a sigh.

"No, Callum. We're not breaking up. You two are mine."

"We're not even together," he counters, and it lashes at my confidence like a barbed whip. "But we'll see," he says before hanging up.

I swallow down the ache squeezing my throat. I'm one

stupid motherfucker if I let these men go without fighting for them. Fighting for my love for them.

Callum's words keep bouncing around in my head. *This isn't Pen's fault. It's yours.*

He's right. This is all my doing. If I had only told Pen about my terrible past, we wouldn't be in this turmoil. And since he's so pissed off at me that he's not willing to pick up my calls, I have to prove it to him—and to Callum—that we are good for each other.

Chapter Twenty-Four

Callum

I take a moment, absorbing the words Dom said to me. *I love you, Callum.*

Those words send a burst of warmth throughout my body. I feel lightheaded, even slightly giddy. Though, I'm not sure if it's from Dom's admission or the nervousness of taking a leap with these men.

I know that we have more than just a physical attraction to each other. When we are together, whether it's just two of us or all three, we don't just have sex. We talk, we laugh, we get to know each other... like couples do, trying to build a connection.

We've formed a bond... been in a relationship all this time and I didn't comprehend that until now.

Why didn't I see that we already *are* together?

The more I roll his declaration around in my head, the more I come to realize that my feelings for these guys are as true as any couple who say they are in love. Like Danny and Tobias. And even if Connor doesn't admit it out loud, he and John are also in love with each other.

Just like them, I'm in love with Dom and Pen. Equally and separately. They have shown me these past months that love—*real* love, not like what I grew up with between my mother and Brian, doesn't hurt. Aside from Dom's default to keeping things close to the vest, that is, which I know he does to protect us. He is going to have to do a lot of explaining about that to Pen.

As if I've conjured him, Pen rushes into the room, gun in hand and eyes wide with fury. "We found Jordan."

I gasp. "Where?"

"He's by the gate. He called and asked me to meet him there," Pen says in a growl.

"I want to go with you," I demand, knowing damn well he won't let me.

"No." He shakes his head. "Stay in the house, and keep the doors locked. Two of Dean's men will be standing guard."

"Pen," I grate out. "I want to look that asshole in the eye when you beat the hell out of him."

"I'm not going to do that. I'm only going to contain him until the cops come." He eyes me warily. "Listen to me. I promise you; you'll get your moment to tell that bastard off, but right now isn't the time. You need to remain here. Promise me that, so I can keep all of my attention on Jordan. Alright?"

"Okay," I concede.

"Once this is over, and the cops arrive, we're leaving. So finish packing." Pen gives me a brief smile and sprints out of the room.

I wait for a minute before walking to the living room. I glance out the window and spot the two men standing by the front entrance. *Good.*

Feeling more secure, I head back into the bedroom to pack. I've just picked up my practice guitar to put it back in the case, when I hear a noise. It wasn't loud, but it was enough to draw my attention. As I walk out to investigate, the front door opens.

"That was pretty quick. Did he give up?" I say, rounding the corner until I come face to face with a man I've never seen before. "Who are you?"

He is wearing dark gray camo, unlike the two guys I saw moments before.

I step back, ready to run when he pulls out a gun and smiles at me. "Don't move, Callum, or I'll put a bullet in the back of your head."

I freeze in place, believing what this guy promises. "Who are you?" I ask, trying to keep the fear out of my voice.

"Don't you know?" His evil smile widens, which has me inwardly quaking, but I try to keep my outward composure as I shake my head no.

"I'm Rick Morrison. Dom's ex-partner from our U.S. Marshal days. What? You haven't heard about me?"

"No, he didn't ever mention you."

Rick walks over to me and I have the completely useless thought that his grin mimics the Joker on *Batman.* Cold and emotionless eyes are fixed on me. As I stand there, unable to move or breathe as he walks toward me, another useless thought flies through my brain. *I really need Pen to give me that self-defense training.* He presses the end of the gun's barrel to my forehead. "Okay. Maybe you remember this. Tell your father to stay out of my business."

I gasp. "You."

"Yes, me." He chuckles.

"Why?" I attempt to hold back my tears, but my vision blurs and Rick's face distorts before me. "Brian has nothing to do with this, with me."

"Well, that's not quite true. But I'm doing you a favor—you know, like a two for one." He shrugs like we're talking about a fucking grocery list.

"Then why me?" I realize it's a stupid question when the puzzle pieces finally begin to slot into place. Dom.

"I'll fill you in when we get on the road." He jabs the gun harder to my skull. "Now move."

"Where are we going?" I ask, as I turn around and face the kitchen area. My brain is scrambling to find a way to escape this crazy bastard. My eyes land on the plates and cast iron frying pan I left on the island, and I realize they are within my reach As I lunge for the frying pan, Rick slams the butt of the gun to my temple and pain rips through my skull. Then everything goes black.

Chapter Twenty-Five

P en

"Where the fuck is he?" I shout, looking past the gate and down the road.

"He was just here. Jordan was standing right there on the other side of the gate. He must have gotten a call, because I saw him bring his phone to his car, but he only talked for a few seconds. Then he got into his car and took off," Fig explains.

"This doesn't make... Fuck." *It's a ruse.* "Callum," I cry out, before jumping into the SUV, along with Fig, and haul ass back to the house. The second I see the men I left to protect Callum lay motionless on the ground, my chest feels like it's been ripped open and I know Callum's in trouble.

I stride inside the house, praying that my gut is wrong,

and that he's safe. But the moment my eyes land on the broken plates, the frying pan laying on the floor of the kitchen and the back slider doors are wide open, someone took Callum.

"Pen," Fig calls me over and points to a piece of notebook paper on the island. "The bastard left us a message."

Without touching it, I read the words out loud. "Want him alive? Tell Dominic Rossetti to come alone to where all this began."

"Jordan was out by the gate—I saw him. So he has to be working with someone." Fig turns from scanning the room to look directly at me. "Do you know what this motherfucker's talking about?" Fig asks, his face a mask of fury as he points to the note.

"I don't, but Dom will."

"Then call Dom, and I'll conference in Tobias and Dean and let them know about Callum." Fig storms outside while I pull out my phone and dial Dom's number, calling him on FaceTime. As much as I'm angry at the asshole, I need to see his face.

"Hey, I'm heading to San Francisco. What's your ETA?" he asks cautiously. His eyes are tired and old Pen would try to soothe him, but I don't have the time or the inclination for niceties.

"Someone took Callum," I reply bluntly.

"What? Who?"

"I don't fucking know. They left a note. *Want him alive? Tell Dominic Rossetti to come alone to where all this began.*"

"Son of a bitch," Dom hisses.

"What the fuck does that mean, Dom?" Then it dawns on me. "This whole time, it was all about you? We were looking at Brian's past, but this jackhole was after *you*?"

"Pen—"

"No, Dom. I don't want you to explain. Just get Callum back," I warn, not ready for his excuses. "I don't care how you do it. And once this is done, we are through."

"I will get Callum back. But I'm making this perfectly clear, you aren't breaking up with me. Once *this* is all done, we'll talk and listen. The three of us."

"It's too late for us—and I'm not arguing with you about it now. We have more pressing matters, like getting Callum back," I rail, not giving a fuck if he doesn't like my denial.

"I don't even know who the fucker is that took him," Dom counters, his storm-filled eyes glaring back at me.

I bite my bottom lip and look up at the ceiling, trying to control my rage. My eyes widen when I spy the smoke detector—we had to turn on its hidden camera when we first arrived. Tobias set it up for extra precautionary measures. "Give me a second and I'll get an image for you."

"How?"

"The security camera in the ceiling," I explain as I make my way to the second bedroom and grab my laptop.

"Shit... Last night," he mutters.

I close my eyes for a second, realizing what he's talking about. When Dom was railing me against the sofa. "Goddamnit. That feed goes straight to Tobias," I utter, feeling my stomach gnarling up even more. "We're never going to hear the end of it."

Dom groans, shaking his head. "Focus."

"I am," I spit out while placing the laptop on the kitchen counter and opening it.

Dom remains quiet while I access the video footage. After a few clicks, I find the time frame I'm looking for and expand the image. "I'm turning my phone camera around so you can see the guy's face."

The second I expand the image, Dom growls, "Mother-fucking son of a bitch. Rick Morrison. This whole time he's been playing me. That asshole played me."

"Who is he?" I ask while memorizing the bastard on the screen.

"He was my partner when I worked for the U.S. Marshals."

"You worked as a marshal?" I practically shriek, then gulp down the acrid taste at the back of throat. I really don't know who Dom is.

What would have been the harm in telling me that he used to be a marshal? It wasn't like he was working for a criminal organization. This whole time, he could have—should have been honest and talked to me about his past. And now look at where we are.

"Pen."

I turn the camera around so he can see my face and the gravity of the situation. "This entire time, it was your ex-partner."

"Yes," he says gravely. "I swear if I had known it was him... I have to call in the feds and the U.S. Marshals. They need to know."

"Why?"

"Because Rick has killed at least six others, and now he's coming after me all because of a case that destroyed both of our lives."

"I wish I could say that I understand that, but I can't. Because I know nothing about that part of your life."

"I'll give you every detail later since I'm no longer under any obligation to keep quiet about the case." He sounds earnest, but it still doesn't justify his lack of communication and secrecy. He's been keeping so much from me.

I'm not sure if I believe him or if I even *want* to believe

Dom. The promises he's dishing out right now are only words. He needs to prove it.

"Dom, all I want is Callum back," I insist. "And I coming with you."

"You're not," Dom declares. "The note says alone and I have no doubt Rick will try to take you out. I can't lose you, Pen."

"Don't you trust me?"

"I do. But I know Rick and he's not one to fuck around."

"I don't care. Tell me where this place is at."

Silence.

"Dom?" Click. I get dead air. "Son of a bitch." He hung up on me.

"Pen," Fig announces from the doorway. "Tobias and Dean are on the line."

"Pen," I hear Tobias's voice.

"Dom knows where Callum is and who took him."

"Who?" That's Dean.

"His ex-partner from the U.S Marshals," I explain. "I pulled up surveillance, and got a still image. And Dom's going after them on his own."

"Shit," Tobias hisses. "Did he tell you where?"

"No," I grate out.

"Send that image to Levi," Dean says. "I have someone on the inside of the marshal's office that has pull."

"On it." I quickly copy the image and send it to Dean's tech guy.

"One more thing. I sent Joel and his group out to scout around the area again," Fig says.

"I'll call Joel for the details," Dean says, then adds, "I'll have Levi track Dom's phone. Once he's down on the ground, we'll find him.

"In the meantime, pack up and then wait for the word," Tobias says, his tone unbending.

"Alright," I convey before hanging up.

I cover my face with both hands, hoping our efforts will be enough. I suck in a deep breath, trying to ward off the tsunami of emotions battering my chest. Callum is out there in the hands of a killer, and Dom is being a dumbass and going after that asshole alone, while I'm here utterly useless.

In an effort to do at least *something* useful, I scroll back through the security camera footage to last night, when Dom and I fucked on the sofa. I pause it when I see Callum standing there, stroking himself off as he watches us. I want to cry.

I'd felt so hopeful last night—like Dom and I were reconnecting... like if we could work through things, I could have both of my men. Now, it's just a reminder of how one-sided our relationship is. Deciding I have enough shit on my plate today, I delete every second of the video from last night with Dom and me in it and then log out and close the laptop.

If Tobias has already seen me getting railed by Dom, so be it. If he hasn't, then it will save a lot of explaining about something that no longer matters.

My head is drowning in information and emotions, and I don't know what to do. Add to that this hurry up and wait scenario—I'm getting righteously pissed off.

"What did you find?" Fig's words penetrate my acerbic thoughts.

I look up and see Fig talking with Joel. "We found what appear to be ATV tracks leading toward the rear of the property. I know there's a dirt access path heading out to the main road about a mile and a half northwest of here."

"Are you sure Callum was on the ATV?" I ask, needing

that confirmation. "What if they left the vehicle and went on foot?"

"No." Joel shakes his head. "From the fresh, deep tread marks, it's looks like the four-by-four had some weight on the back end. We trailed it about half way until we took out the drone and saw the abandoned ATV on the side of the road. The drone video was clear enough to see tread marks on the road. Pete thinks they got into a van. And..." Joel hesitates. "Some of the tread marks were distorted by two parallel drag marks—like the heels of shoes."

"God damn it! Are you sure?"

"Pete's one of the best damn trackers we have, aside from me," Fig conveys with a smirk. "I trust his word."

"How long do you think they've been gone?" I ask.

"No more than twenty minutes—thirty tops," Joel says. "Why?"

"Let's go after them," Fig declares, yanking a vehicle fob from his pocket.

"No. We need to call Tobias. Going after them will only waste energy and time we don't have," I advise, pulling out my phone and dialing Tobias's number, putting the call on speaker.

"Got something?" Tobias's tone has a sharp edge to it. I'm familiar with that tone, and it's one you don't want aimed your way.

"Joel's team found ATV tracks. The trail led to a back road where it appears they took off in a van about thirty minutes ago," I quickly explain.

"I'll relay that to Dean. But it's out of our hands now, Pen. The U.S. Marshals and the feds are involved. They pretty much told us to back off and they will handle Rick and retrieve Callum for us."

"What about Dom? He knows where Rick's heading," I say.

Dom would be in the crossfire between Rick, the feds and the U.S. Marshals.

"Like Dean explained, Levi is going to track Dom's phone once he gets off the jet. While we wait, we have some time to prepare," Tobias states.

"I can't just sit here, Tobias. You wouldn't be idle if Danny was in the same situation," I say, my throat aching from the tightness there.

"Then gather your stuff and head our way. I'll keep you updated while you're on the road."

Soon after locking the place up, we haul ass out of Tobias's place. We cautiously exceed the speed limit as we make our way toward San Fran. I thanked Fig for taking the driver's seat, as I wouldn't be able to concentrate on the road while my mind is drowning in what ifs.

I know I keep saying we're done, but what if I really do lose Dom? Or Callum? Jesus—both of them? How could I continue to live without these men? Without their love, without their laughter, without their solace, I'll be nothing more than a shell.

As I wage internal war in a search for the answers, my heart is the organ that's being fractured in two. As much as I keep promising myself that I'll break it off with Dom, deep down, I can't stand the idea of leaving him—or seeing Callum walk away from us. I love those men equally. No matter how frustrating Dom can be.

He did promise to explain about his life, and I hope he follows through on that, but my only concern right now is getting both him and Callum back, each in one, uninjured piece.

For Christ sakes, I'm tearing up. As I quickly wipe the

evidence away with the back of my hand, my cell phone rings. I glance down, hoping it's one of my men's name popping up on the screen, and sigh. Just when I didn't think this day could get any shittier.

I grudgingly remember my promise to Ron, accept the call, and put the phone to my ear. "Mom."

"Honey, I hope I'm not bothering you."

"I'm a little busy right now," I say briskly. It's not a lie.

"Okay. Then I'll make it quick. If you have some time, I'll be in San Francisco in three weeks. Can we meet up for lunch or dinner and talk... Please?" Her plea hits me square in the chest, cramming itself in with the rest of my unsettled emotions.

I'm about to say no, then again remember what Ron made me promise. "Sure. Let me know when you arrive and we can plan something."

"Oh—okay. Great. I'll call you then." Her voice lightens, and she ekes out a little laugh. "Okay, Pen. Talk to you soon. Love you."

My breath hitches in the back of my throat at her declaration. I don't know how to respond.

"Okay."

Right before she hangs up, I say, "I love you too."

"Talk to you soon."

I then hang up, and I realize my face is wet.

"Don't worry," Fig says evenly. "I won't tell a soul."

I look over at the man, who I always find a little strange, especially the odd things that come out of his mouth. Yet, something about the man encourages me to openly confess my feelings.

"My mom..."

"Don't have to say a word. I know—been there and have a

t-shirt to prove it. Now all we need to do is get your guys back to you."

I turn my attention to the window while swallowing down the boulder-size lump in my throat.

"I can't lose them, Fig," I profess in a whisper.

It's the truth. I don't know if I can survive without them.

"You won't." His steely confidence bolsters my determination to stay hopeful.

Chapter Twenty-Six

D^{om}

Hanging up on Pen might not have been a smart move, but there's no way I'm having him come with me and be in the line of Rick's fire. That bastard has nothing to lose and will shoot Pen dead without thinking.

With Callum in Rick's hands, he would then hold all of the cards. Callum's life is on the line. Adding Pen into the mix would only rile Rick up and make the situation worse.

My mind races at how to approach Rick. How to enter the trailer park where all this began, without being seen. How much I'm going to enjoy wrapping my hands around the fucker's neck for taking what's mine.

"Jesus, Callum." I rub the back of my neck in frustration.

Exhausted and anxious for the jet to hit the tarmac, I

scroll through my texts and see the number Rick first texted me from.

I still don't know how he fooled me. Rick made it appear that he had turned into a drunk and a junky. There were so many empty bottles and cans lying all around his apartment. Then there were the burned tin foils, spoons and discarded needles on the table. Visually, it was easy for me to believe he was an addict. Wait—was that even his apartment?

And that person that supposedly attacked him? Suddenly, I remember Rick's clean fingernails...

Everything was a fucking lie. *Christ, I'm such a gullible idiot.*

My eyes study the number until my finger, almost of its own volition, taps the call button.

I suck in a breath as the phone rings. Then the call hits dead air. I don't say anything, just listen for a beat.

"I knew you'd call me," Rick eventually says with an insidious chuckle.

"Why are you doing this, Rick?" I try to keep my voice even, but my rage is seeping through my words.

"Why do you think?" The incredulousness in his voice has my hackles up.

"I don't know, I can't read your fucking mind," I bite out. I'm not playing games with him anymore.

More chuckling from the other end. Then I hear a whimper. *Callum.*

"If you hurt one hair on that man's head, I swear there's nowhere you can hide," I growl in warning.

"How sweet. You see, Dom. You should have died with Jacob like you were supposed to."

"Like I was supposed to?" I repeat in confusion. Thinking back to that night, it was a scramble—trying to get

Jacob out of that trailer as the bullets were turning the mobile home into Swiss cheese. But we only had seconds before the killers made their way inside and shot Jacob.

"I took the bullet that was meant for you," he rants. "And now look at me. No wife or son. No career. No connection to her family."

What the hell is he talking about? What's this got to do with *her* family?

"We were lucky to be alive, Rick." I try to target his sensible side, hoping he'll see reason. "And Callum isn't involved in this. Never was. Let him go."

But he refuses to listen.

"Do you understand that you don't deserve to live, Dom? That killing you isn't enough? I have to take what *you* love the most. Only then will you have an inkling of my pain."

"What about those feds you killed?" My gut instinct is telling me that Rick is also behind the murders I learned about in Joust's office. But why?

Silence meets my ears.

"Rick—"

"Fuck off, Dom. You're not hearing me. You should have died with that twink. If Victor Mastov's man had had good aim and nailed *you* between the eyes instead of shooting me in the chest, we wouldn't be here."

"Victor Mastov?" I grit out as my fury turns into an inferno. "You. *You* were the snitch?"

"Give that man a cigar. Yeah. I had no choice. Either I did it or I'd lose my family." The heinous laughter on the other end of the call is like a knife gutting me from neck to sternum. "But I lost them anyway."

"You son of a bitch. You sold us out—and for what?"

"Lots and lots of money, and for the love of my woman. You still haven't figured it out? I've been in deep with them for a long, long time. Family is everything. And I would have kept mine, if the job had been done correctly. And now I get a second chance to make things right. And you're the last loose end to tie up, Dom."

"You killed all those agents and for what?" I'm gut-punched and utterly shocked by Rick's confession.

"Victor gave me no choice. Clean up my mess, or die and never see my kid again. What would you have me do?" he asks. "Now you know. Tick tock, Dom. Better hurry up. You do want to see your boyfriend alive one more time, don't you?"

"Rick!" I scream, but I'm yelling at dead air. He fucking hung up. I try redialing but it goes straight to voicemail.

Think—damn it. Think. I unbuckle the seat belt and get up to pace the aisle. The harder I think, the faster I pace. I need a plan. If Callum and I are to come out of this alive, I'm going to need help.

Jesus-fucking-Christ. If I heard Rick correctly, he married into the Mastov family.

Why didn't Joust know this? But then, knowing the bastard, he knew and kept that information close to the vest.

I pull up another phone number—the one I didn't think I'd ever use again, and tap it and call.

"Rossetti," he answers in his usual stoic tone.

"How long?"

"How long what?"

"How long have you known that Rick was married into the Mastov family."

"About a week. How did you find out?"

That's bullshit. Greg's lying, but I don't focus on it. "I just talked to Rick."

"Do you know where he's heading?"

"Royal Oaks Mobile Home Park," I say with malice. "So

when were you going to tell me it was Rick? This entire time, he's been after my men and you didn't say one fucking word."

"We weren't sure—not until he took Callum Fitz as a hostage," Joust says with a bit more empathy.

"Liar. I know you have ears, eyes and your nose all over the damn place. You knew he was coming after me. I'm telling you right now, if Callum gets harmed, I'll make sure the entire world knows who was at fault. You."

"Threats don't work on me," Joust grates out.

"It doesn't matter. You handled this poorly, just like you handled Jacob's case poorly. He died because you and the feds didn't secure the witness. You let a member of a syndicate family work as the bodyguard for a witness who was going to testify against that syndicate. How fucked up is that? It's your fault, Greg, that you didn't look into your own people." I let out all the aggression that's been pent-up for years.

"Did you know Brian Fitz came to us six months ago, clueing us in on Rick's connections to Victor Mastov? Did you know Brian Fitz is also associated with the Mastovs?"

Well, that's news to me, but I'm not all that shocked to hear it, since Brian doesn't know how to keep his nose clean. "I know now."

"I told your friend, Dean Harper, to stay out of this and we'll get Callum back, unharmed," Joust explains. "Keep your distance, Dom. I want you out of this mess."

"Bullshit," I shout into the phone. "Listen to me. Rick's expecting me go there. If you show up instead, I know for a fact he's going to kill Callum and I can't let you do that."

"Goodbye, Rossetti." Joust hangs up and I see nothing but red.

I throw my phone across the plane, and the device

crashes against the wall. Once I clear my head, I pick it up. The screen is shattered and the cell isn't working.

No matter, I know how to get to Royal Oaks. The second the jet lands, I grab a rental and head straight to the trailer park.

Fuck Joust if he doesn't like it. I know Rick well enough. He was my partner for many years. If I don't show up, he'll kill Callum. And I can't let that happen.

If anything, I'd give up my life for Callum's, and I wouldn't regret it because I know he would still have Pen.

Chapter Twenty-Seven

Callum

I don't know how long I've been out cold, but the moment I move, my entire body aches with pain. I stealthily open my eyes to gauge where I am, but that is a mistake. I close them again as my temples begin to pound in a steady rhythm, matching the pounding of my heart.

Breathe in. Breathe out.

Attempting to remain calm, I open my eyes again and turn my head to see where exactly I am. I quickly realize that my legs are bound at my ankles and my arms are tied behind my back—and fucking A but my arm below the split hurts like a bitch. Shifting my head slowly to the right, I see a fragment of light coming through a broken window blind.

Focusing on it, I follow the beam to a closed door, which isn't that far from where I'm lying... I'm on a mattress. I sniff and recoil from the nasty smell. Mildew and dirt, and something else I'm afraid to name, penetrate my senses.

I groan in protest, but immediately tamp down the sound by clamping my mouth tight.

Too late. I hear heavy footsteps. The door swings open and a light blinks on, momentarily blinding me.

"Well, well, well. You're finally up." Rick bends down until he is eye level with me. His face is so close to mine, if he came any closer, I'd bite his nose off. "What? Nothing to say?"

"Fuck you," I seethe.

"No, I'm not gay." He chuckles as though he made a joke. "But if I were, *I'd* be fucking *you*. Do you want some? Because I *could* accommodate you," he says with a wink.

"I'd rather die than let you touch me," I grit out.

"Don't worry, precious. Your man is on his way, and once he's here, you can have him. Hell, you two can be together forever for all I care—and oh, by the way, this next bit of information is out of courtesy. Your father won't see the light of day once I'm done with you and Dom."

"My father?" I choke out.

What did you do, Brian?

"Yeah. He fucked over Victor Mastov. Stole money and drugs that weren't his. And now Victor wants him gone."

"How much?" I don't know why I care, but I'm curious.

"Two mill, and some change."

I have no words. This proves that Brian was a loser back then, and he still is. But do I want him dead? No—for my mother's sake. She still loves the bastard.

"Hmm. Nothing to say?" Rick asks, a smirk plastered on his face.

I remain quiet, watching the psycho prick in front of me.

He chuckles, stands and walks out of what I now think is

a bedroom. Rick left the light on, so I can see what's around me. It takes me several attempts, but I'm finally able to sit up.

The binding on my wrists is tight. But with all the twisting around it took to sit, the rope Rick used loosened a bit and I'm able to wiggle my hands and get the blood flowing back into my fingers.

I glance down at the mattress and grimace at the sight. It looks even worse than it smells. Dark patches of mold and unrecognizable stains have me scooting away from those spots.

Voices from the other room make me pause and listen—apparently Rick isn't alone. I try to identify the other voice—it could be Jordan, but I'm not sure. I listen and catch a few words, and the name Victor is loud and clear. My guess is that whoever Victor is, he's sending people—and Rick isn't happy about it, judging from his shouting and the sounds of glass being smashed and stuff being thrown around.

It occurs to me that maybe it's a good thing Rick isn't happy. This news will keep him off-kilter. And when Dom gets here, he'll put this dog down. On the other hand, if Victor's men arrive here first, Dom and I are at a much bigger risk of dying in their hands.

"Hurry, Dom. Hurry."

Chapter Twenty-Eight

P en

"We lost him," Tobias informs me.

"What do you mean you lost him?" I rake my nails along my scalp, letting the bite of pain help center me.

"Levi said the last location he has for Dom was on the jet. Dean called the pilot, who informed him that Dom got off the plane and headed to one of the rental agencies."

"Then how are we going to find out where he's going?" I ask, my frustration gaining momentum.

"We don't need to. Levi found Dom's last case and where it ended."

"And?" I sniped. I'm too far gone to care anymore if I piss off Tobias.

"I know you're stressed. We are too. So I'm going to let

that fly. But before I tell you where, what are you going to do once you find out?"

"I'm going after my men. And you would do the same, Tobias," I declare.

"I would, but you're forgetting one thing. You have people. So I suggest you wait for us and then we can regroup and go in together."

"That's your answer?" I can't believe he's suggesting that. He'd be the first to jump in without waiting for any one of us. "No, Tobias. I can't wait."

"Alright," he sighs. "Dom's heading to Royal Oaks Mobile Home Park. It's in Orland, California."

"Then we're heading that way," I declare.

"We? Is Fig with you?"

"I'm here," Fig answers. "And Joel's with us."

"Okay. Dean gave us a go. Said to clean house if you have to."

I glance at Fig, who's smiling, and I'm far from confused on the term.

"Got it," he says, not losing his grin.

"Pen. Keep your head low and if the feds and the marshals show first, let them do their jobs."

"Stay safe." I hear Danny's voice in the background. "Don't die!"

"Babe," Tobias scolds him, and they begin to argue when he explains to Danny what cleaning house means. Not wanting to hear it, I hang up the call.

"If I need to kill to protect us, I'll do it with prejudice," Fig says stoically.

"Damn. This means Jordan too?" I ask

Fig nods, grimacing. "If I have no choice."

"Alright. Joel, text Pete on the destination while I get an address and put it in the GPS."

Once I add the trailer park into the system, it shows we're two hours away. I hope we get there in time. And before all hell breaks loose.

Chapter Twenty-Nine

om

I park along the east side of the massive abandoned property, opposite to the spot where the old trailer once stood—the mobile home that was the safe house for the witness Rick and I had protected. Jacob Cunningham.

After Jacob was murdered, the entire community was outraged and the residents of Royal Oaks moved out. And now the place is a ghost town.

As I creep along the edge of the tall grasses and massive hedges around the perimeter, the overgrowth will make it a little easier to go in undetected.

I'm glad to see that the place is still abandoned—I won't have innocent people to worry about.

I quietly work my way through the brambles and chest-high weeds until I'm within shooting distance of the trailer, then I hunch behind a copse of out-of-control honeysuckle bushes. I plan to stay here until dusk disappears so I can go in under the dark of night.

As I'm crouched down low, I see activity around the mobile home. Two black SUVs pull up and seven men get out. This close, I can see that six are dressed in expensive suits, and each one is holding a gun. The seventh man is much smaller, and he doesn't have a gun. He's turned away from me, being pulled toward the trailer by the two men leading the group, and I can't make out who he is without seeing his face. One thing I'm sure of, though, is that he's not Callum. The suits are talking, but I can't hear them clearly from this distance.

The way they are dressed and the fact that they are holding guns, makes me think these are Victor Mastov's men. Guess I'm don't have to wait until dark.

Rick did say that he wants back in with Victor, and in order for that to happen, he has to finish me off. But then why all the men? It doesn't make sense to have this much fire power show up, unless Rick didn't know they were coming.

The two men dragging the smaller guy head inside while the other four surround the mobile home.

I'm tempted to move, get closer to see if: one, Callum's alright, and two, if these men are still talking. But where is a safe spot? I scan the area and spot a dilapidated storage shed, small but big enough to hide my bulky frame.

I carefully move away from the honeysuckle and make my way around to the rear of the shed. With my back to it and my gun in my hand, I hear quiet voices coming close.

"He's a dumbass. He has no clue that Victor wanted him dead even back then," one says, lighting a cigarette.

The other laughs. "I don't think he realizes what we are

doing here. We only need to tie up this end and we're out of here."

"It's better this way. Once that Dom guy comes, we can pick off both of them and then negotiate a price for the bassist."

"I like Warrior Black's music. It would be a shame if we have to kill him off," the one with the cigarette says. "And I had tickets for this year's Rocktoberfest in Black Rock."

"I doubt Victor will let him go, unless we go in and cover his head so he doesn't see our faces."

"He already has. Tomas and Del are inside there."

"Oh, that's right."

Shit. I need to move fast and get Callum out of here. As I get ready to shoot the duo, I catch movement to the right of me. Even in the muted light of dusk, I know that body well.

Pen.

Four men are with him, all of them moving stealthily toward me. They split up—Pen comes to me, while two head in one direction toward the far side of the trailer and the other two go toward the two numb-nuts who are still talking.

Pen moves until he's squatting by my feet, smiling up at me like a ray of sunshine. "Miss me?" he whispers.

The relief at seeing his grinning face fills me with so much love, that it overrides my fear of him being involved in this.

"Babe, as much as I love seeing you on your knees for me, get up here," I say so quietly that I'd be surprised if Pen hears the words.

He swiftly stands, leans in, brushes his lips to my ear and murmurs, "I'll want that apology in many forms and as many times as I need it." He kisses my cheek and looks patiently into my eyes.

I wrap one arm around him and pull Pen in, chest to

chest, and whisper, "As many times as I need to. Now let's go get our guy?" He nods, understanding we are here *together* to save Callum.

We turn toward the trailer as shit starts to go down. Fig, Jordan and Dean's men neutralize Victor's men outside the trailer. Then gunfire erupts inside the mobile home.

"Callum," Pen says in a low rush.

"The four are down," I hear Fig call out. "Go get Callum."

"I lead," I tell Pen, and with another nod, we head to the door of the trailer.

We creep up to the small porch, where the aluminum frame of a screen door is sagging wide open, its mesh material long gone. As my foot lands on the step, the inner door flies open and Brian, with Callum in his arms, comes hurrying out of the trailer. *Shit! Brian must have been the smaller man dragged in.*

"Take him," Brian hisses as he stands Callum in front of me. I glance down at Callum, whose wrists and ankles are bound, and wrap my left arm around him to hold him upright.

"Brian," Callum pleads. "Don't go back inside."

"If I don't kill him, he'll come after you again," Brian says as he turns around to head back in, but Rick is standing right in the threshold, a gun in his hand. He's aiming at our little group, although I'm not sure who his target is—Callum, Pen, me, or Brian.

"Rick," I begin to say, but the bastard pulls the trigger twice before I finish his name.

Brian screams, leaps to stand in front of Callum, and both bullets hit the man in the chest.

"Dad," Callum cries out. But my focus is on Rick. I pull

the trigger on my gun and hit him dead center in the chest, while Pen shoots him in the head.

And then chaos reigns as we are surrounded by feds and marshals.

Chapter Thirty

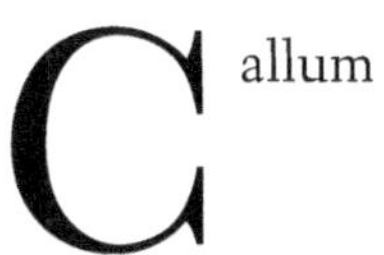

allum

It's been two weeks since the shootout happened in the trailer park. I will never forget it. What surprises me the most is that I haven't had any nightmares.

Despite the fear of being killed, seeing Rick shoot Jordan point blank right in front of me, watching the fight between Rick and the two goons, and the shock of seeing my father there, I've been able to sleep. I'm not even having nightmares any longer about the attack in Evergreen.

I believe that is because of what my father did for me. He saved me. Brian literally gave his life for mine, and that knowledge seems to have healed my wounds and traumas. He might not have been the best father growing up, but he proved to me that he loved me.

Today was his funeral. We buried him at Queen of

Heavens cemetery. During the graveside service, my mother stood on my right, Pen was on my left, and Dom stood behind Pen and me. My best friends were there, too, of course, as were Tobias, John, Fig, Dante and Dean, along with the rest of Harper Security. I was surprised to see Lyric there too.

Ron couldn't come, but Dean hugged my mother and then—awkwardly, me on Ron's behalf. I was glad Ron decided to conserve his strength and not make the trip to Chicago. The day was a hot one, and Dean was busy helping Dante, whose four-inch heels kept sinking into the plush grass of the cemetery.

With all the people who mean so much to me there, I was able to get through the day and support my mother. Her friends had also arranged a lovely reception for us, where we could share memories of the times when Brian was a good father and a wonderful husband.

We took my mother back to her house and then grabbed our bags. Her best friend was staying with her tonight since Dom, Pen and I had decided we'd stay at a hotel. We needed the alone time together.

Though, it has been a whirlwind. We'd each been debriefed separately, Dom multiple times. They'd had to do an autopsy on Brian to determine whose bullets had killed him, and then there was the rigamarole of getting his body from California to Chicago and planning the funeral. Dom's friend from Chicago Sentinel had brought Mum to us in California, where I let her fuss over me for a few days as a distraction from the shit with Brian—she went into full Mama Bear mode when she learned I'd taken another hit to my concussed head.

I went back to Evergreen by myself to grab the things I'd left behind when we fled and to put the house on the market, something I felt I had to do for closure.

With everything going on, I'd barely seen Dom and Pen. We'd texted and called each other, but what we really need to say can only be said in person. There's so much we have to unpack: what happened from the time I was attacked in Evergreen, the arguments between Pen and Dom, and then the big unknown—where we three stand in the relationship.

Now, as we position ourselves in different parts of the hotel room, silence fills the space.

I glance at Pen first. His arms are folded across his chest and his attention is to the ceiling. Then I look at Dom, whose posture mirrors Pen's, except his eyes are on the floor.

"For fuck's sake. Someone talk," I say from my perch on the bed.

Both men look at me at the same time, but neither of them says anything.

"You know what? I'm leaving. I had a crappy day and watching both of you Debbie-downers makes me feel even more unhappy." I get up from the bed, grab my overnight bag and head to the door.

I don't make it four steps before thick arms wrap around me from behind. "I'm sorry," Dom says.

"I'm not the one you should say sorry to," I reply over my shoulder.

"Babe, we talked," Pen says, his hand cupping my face. "Dom apologized many times. And he will keep apologizing until I say otherwise." A small smirk slides across his face.

"Then what's with the silence?" I demand. "I thought you two were working things out, but right now you aren't acting any differently than you were back at Tobias's lake house."

"We're waiting to see what you need. Today was a tough day for you and your mom. We don't want to come after you like crazed sex fiends," Dom explains, then tucks his chin close to my neck and kisses my ear.

"What if I want you two to be crazed sex fiends? What if that's what I need?"

"Then Callum, if that's what you want, we aim to please," Pen says with the kind of smile that songs are written about. He leans in, pulling me from Dom's arms and kisses me, long and thoroughly. His touch has my heart pumping and my dick hardening in my slacks.

"But we still need to have a talk," Dom interjects, and Pen and I groan.

"What?" I pull out of Pen's arms and sit on the edge of the bed, facing the two men.

"We love you," Dom begins to say.

"We want you in our lives—always—the three of us," Pen adds. "Together."

"We just need to make sure you're good and ready for this relationship." A little bit of Dom's insecurities are peeking through, and I love that he now feels like he can show that side of himself. Just like Pen can.

"Callum Fitz, would you like to be in a committed relationship with us, Pennington Gallagher and Dominic Rossetti?"

I contemplate for all of five seconds before my men are on me. Kissing me, loving me.

"Yes, I want to be in a relationship with you both. Now can we fuck, please?" I plead with a pout.

Neither hesitate. They begin stripping out of their suits, which leaves me to watch my men as they give me a striptease. Once they are down to their birthday suits, I take off my clothes and we three head into the large shower.

When we're clean and my body has been thoroughly stretched by Pen, Dom leans in and kisses me and then Pen, before offering, "As penance, I want you and Pen to both fuck me tonight."

My eyes go wide, and so do Pen's. "Are you sure?" I ask, because I like being the bottom. But if this is for Pen, I will happily switch.

"You've never bottomed, Dom," Pen says.

"Yes, I have. It's been years, but I trust you both to take care of me."

Pen wraps a hand on the back of Dom's neck, draws him in and kisses him hard. "I love you."

"I love you, too," Dom utters against his lips.

They turn to me, pull me in and say at the same time, "We love you."

"And I love you both." I kiss each of them with equal passion.

We move from the bathroom, still wet, to the king-size bed. The starched white sheets cling to our damp bodies, but none of us care.

With tangled limbs, we touch, taste, and grind on each other until we need more. I need more.

Pen grabs the lube while I bend over and take Dom's cock into my mouth. God, I love the taste of his skin and his precum that's flowing heavily from the tip. I suck him back as far as I can while using my hand to cup his fuzzy balls.

"Fuck, baby—your mouth. Oh, God—yes, Pen. Give me two fingers. I need it."

As Pen stretches Dom's ass, I pop off of Dom's dick, leaving it slick with saliva. I turn—my back to Dom's front, and move until his thick length is nudging my hole.

"Don't move, Dom, and keep your hands to yourself," I look over my shoulder and order, repeating what he said to me the only other time we three made love.

Dom groans but does as I ask. I wiggle a little more until

his head slides past my first ring of muscle, then I pause, letting myself adjust to his size.

"Are you ready for three?" Pen whispers to Dom.

"Yes," he utters and then moans loudly as Pen penetrates him at the same time I push back until I'm fully impaled on Dom's dick.

"I'm not going to last," Dom admits with a groan. "Fuck—fuck me already."

"We have all night," I admit and begin to move faster.

"Hell yeah, we do," Pen echoes as he slides his cock into Dom.

"You're punishing me," Dom moans.

"Yes, we are," I say and bounce my ass against him, as Pen thrusts in counterpoint to my movements, so that Dom is being impaled as my ass is swallowing his length whole.

We are connected in so many ways. Our bodies, our minds and our hearts. There are no words—no songs that could truly capture what I feel for these two men. The depth of my affection for them goes beyond anything I can express —any song lyrics I think of.

The journey we've taken to get here may have been longer than we all anticipated, but looking back, I wouldn't change a thing. I'm so grateful for every step we've taken together, and for the bond we've built—it's something I'll carry with me always.

"I can't wait any longer. Callum," Pen groans. "Stroke yourself."

"Yes," I utter, trying to match the rhythm with Pen as he speeds up and drives deep into Dom's ass.

But in true Dominic Rossetti fashion, he takes over. He clamps his hands on my shoulders and begins to move his hips. I brace one hand on the wall in front of me while jack myself.

Dom's drills me faster and harder, all the while Pen is railing Dom just as roughly.

"I can't—" I keen out, losing the rest of my words as my entire body becomes electrified and I come immediately.

Pen groans low and guttural, and Dom thrusts falters, before he growls out, "Fuck."

I don't know how long we stay connected, Dom's heavy frame leaning against me, but I see Pen out of my periphery. Then Dom's weight is gone, and he slowly pulls out of me.

"Baby," Dom says before kissing Pen. He then reaches for me and leads me to the shower. We three barely fit the space, but none of us minds.

Once clean, we end up back in bed, where we kiss and touch each other, absorbing the love.

I take a slow deep inhale, breathing in the scent of our lovemaking, and I know this is where I'm supposed to be. In the arms of my two men.

Epilogue

C allum

"Are you ready to hit the stage?" Dante asks me through the lighted makeup mirror in the back room.

"Yes," I say as I try to cover up the hickeys on my neck. *Damn you, Dom, for doing this right before Rocktoberfest.*

"Hell yeah, he is," Danny announces as he adjusts the silver lamé vest he has on, which matches his painted-on jeans, and gives me a hip bump. "How much time do we have?" he asks Dante, who is fixing their lipstick.

"We have an hour and a half before we head to the stage."

"I can't believe we hit the primetime spot," Bobby chimes in as he picks out his afro. He glances in the wall mirror and then at us. "Too much?"

"Not at all," Danny says as he swipes his lips with the latest flavored lip balm.

"You do you," Dante chimes in. "And why not the prime-time? I worked hard getting you guys that spot. Warrior Black is going to kick ass tonight, too."

"We always do," Rafe says as he sticks his head into the room. "Did anyone see Lyric?"

"I thought he was up front by the driver." I point to the front of the bus.

Shortly after my father's funeral, Lyric showed up at the San Francisco house and stayed. None of us had dared to ask Dante what they'd said to convince Lyric to come back, but we're grateful. Having a medical person on staff has come in handy more times than we'd expected—thank God it's been for minor stuff. No more gunshot wounds. I hope.

"Why?" Danny asks with a smile. "Do you have a booboo?"

"Fuck off, Danny. John wants him."

"John cut his pinky finger," Connor announces, as he slides past Rafe, who moves back toward the hallway. Then Connor plants his ass on my lap and drops an arm over my shoulder. "How are you, Crocodile Dundee? Ready to play?"

"Why aren't you worried for your man?" I ask, trying to push my friend off of me.

"Because he deserves what he got. He shouldn't be playing with knives," Connor says so nonchalantly. "Besides, John's fine. He doesn't need stitches. Only a small bandage, and I already gave him one."

"Well, I'm glad—now get your bony ass off my legs. You're cutting off the circulation."

"Whatever, dick," Connor flips me a middle finger.

"Play nice," Dante declares, eyeballing us.

"We always play nice." Bobby pops a tiny sucker into his mouth.

"We need to chat about your problem with sugar." Dante points to Bobby's mouth and frowns.

"I'm weening myself off. It's a small one." Bobby pulls the sucker out of his mouth. "See?"

Danny shushes us. "Listen… What's that noise?"

I take a moment. "Wait. Is that a moan?"

We look around us, like we are counting who's in the room. Everyone but Rafe is here with us.

Then Bobby busts out laughing. "I knew it. Someone owes me money."

"Shit," Connor says and hands him a twenty.

"Who is that?" I ask.

"Who do you think?" Danny adds.

I look around the room again before asking, "Rafe?"

"With who?" Connor stands, determination to find out written across his face, but Dante stops him.

"Don't worry about it. Get ready and I'll take care of it," they declare and leave the room.

"Who can it be?" Danny looks at Bobby, but our keyboardist shakes his head no. I have a feeling he knows, since he hangs out with Rafe almost all the time. I'd put my money on Lyric, although I could be wrong.

About forty minutes before we are to climb onto the stage, Rafe rejoins us as we all head to the food tent. With the tight scheduling today, none of us got a chance to eat, and we want to grab a bite before we work up a sweat on stage.

Walking into the food tent, check out what's on the menu, before we fill our plates. As we go, we chat with some of the friends we've made since we started playing at Rocktoberfest and finally take a seat at a empty table.

Dom, Pen and the rest of our security team have come with us and stationed themselves around the table we are sitting at. I glance over at my guys and smile. They both wink at me before they slide masks of indifference on their faces.

"Taking it a bit much, aren't they?" a guy says at the table next to us.

"Do I know you?" I ask, angling my body in his direction. I don't think I know this man, but his face is familiar.

"No, but I know you," he says with an oily smile, pulls out a small camera from under his shirt and begins taking pictures of me and the entire band.

"Get the hell out of here. No reporters are allowed in here," one of the event's security men says as he grabs the guy, confiscates his camera, and then pushes him away from us and out of the tent.

"Who is that?" Connor whispers.

"That dude is trouble. He was caught taking pictures of another band while they were sleeping on their bus last night," Fig explains, shaking his head.

"Thank Christ we arrived early this morning," I mutter, since I have had enough bullshit to last me a life time. And last night? Danny let me have the back bedroom on the tour bus, and Dom, Pen and I got into some heavy petting. I can't imagine having pictures circulated of us in compromising positions. It's all I need—on top of the crap that has already happened.

Dom and Pen reach my side. "What did he say to you?" Dom asks.

"He said he knows me—or us, I'm not sure."

"Don't worry, we'll take care of it and make sure he doesn't come near the band," Dom adds.

"They should have better security around the tent where the groups hang out." Pen frowns. Then they each firmly place a hand against my lower back.

I roll my eyes at their not-so-subtle possessive move.

"It's time, boys," Dante announces, clapping their hands. "Are you ready?"

"We are ready," Danny throws out, high-fiving each of us. His enthusiasm is catching and by the time we get on stage, the fans have caught it too and are screaming and chanting *Warrior Black.*

We play a mix of some of our earlier songs and some from the current album, and then Danny tells them we have a surprise for them.

We all agreed we'd give our fans at Rocktoberfest a hint of what's to come, and picked three songs from the new album that's due out next spring. One of them is the song I wrote at Tobias's lake house, which I called *Three Times the Love.* The second is one Danny and Connor wrote, and the third is one Bobby wrote a while ago called *Addiction.*

All three songs end up being smashing successes, and an encore later, we come off the stage, sweat slicked, hungry and, I have to admit, damn horny. Especially after Danny let me sing my song, and I had Pen and Dom's full attention.

They know the song is for them—they heard it while we were recording it in the studio. But I also explained what the song is about to the audience tonight. So now the world knows about us and our love.

The thunderous exhale of the crowd—their acceptance lifting me higher in this world of music, friends, and the two loves of my life.

As I climb off the stage, I see Rafe looking around. Then his attention lands on Lyric, who's all kinds of red. I don't know, but I have a feeling the next whirlwind coming at us is already here.

The End

A Note from CJ

Dear Reader,

I hoped you enjoyed reading Tone Deaf, book three in the Warrior Black Series, which is part of TL Travis's Road to Rocktoberfest 2024 world.

Callum, Dom and Pen gave me a run for my patience. But I loved every moment of writing their journey into finding their happiness. I look forward to what's in the future for them.

And who knows, maybe the next book will be announced when and who in my newsletter. If you haven't already join me, to see what I have in store for you the link is below.

Want to be notified when my next book comes out, click the link. www.cjbarloweauthor.com/newsletter

All my best,

CJ

About CJ

CJ Barlowe is an author of gay romance and the alter ego of CJ Warrant. CJ writes hard edge romance with all the feels. There's always a happily ever after, even though there's casualties of the heart. Addicted to coffee, loves her family and great friends, CJ's stories will always lead you in the mood for love.

For more about CJ and her books, join her facebook group, CJ Barlowe's MM romance Clan. You can also follow her on instagram and TikTok.

linktr.ee/cjbarloweauthor

Also by CJ Barlowe

<u>Warrior Black Series:</u>

Killer Notes

Beyond The Stix

<u>Lumber-Bear Shifter Series</u>

Coming Soon

www.ingramcontent.com/pod-product-compliance
Lightning Source LLC
Chambersburg PA
CBHW070458300726

48975CB00007B/2225